CARTEL PUBLICATIONS

PRESENTS

Shyt List

And A Child Shall Lead Them

a novel by **Reign**

PUBLISHER'S NOTE:
This book is a work of fiction. Names, characters, businesses,
Organizations, places, events and incidents are the product of the
Author's imagination or are used fictionally. Any resemblance of
Actual persons, living or dead, events, or locales are entirely coincidental.

Library of Congress Control Number: 2009913365
ISBN: 0-9823913-8-2
ISBN 13: 978-0-9823913-8-9
Cover Design: Davida Baldwin www.oddballdsgn.com
Editor: Advanced Editorial Services
Graphics: Davida Baldwin
www.thecartelpublications.com
First Edition

Printed in the United States of America

**THIS BOOK IS DEDICATED TO THOSE WHO
LIKE A LITTLE SOMETHING DIFFERENT**

ENJOY

What up Fam!

I'm surprised you readin' this letter first. The way some of ya'll been geekin' for this book, I just knew ya'll was goin' dive right into it, lol. Seriously, on behalf of The Cartel Publications, let me just take a few ticks to show our gratitude. I've said it before, and mean it each and every time. We appreciate you from our soul. All we do at The Cartel Publications is for you.

The wait is over. Yvonna is back and she got help, but did it work? Is she a normal member of society now or still just as crazy as cat shit? I'ma let ya'll find out for yourself. But before I let you get to it, you know we gotta pay our dues as we do in all our novels to a literary vet or up and coming star. All I gotta say is two words:

"Jason Poole"

Jason C. Poole, one of the most vicious authors in this industry, is who the Cartel Publications pays homage to in this book. He is the author of such novels as, "Larceny"; "Convict's Candy" and the Cartel's own, "Victoria's Secret". Jason is not only a phenomenal author; he's one of the realest niggas I've ever known. I haven't met a dude this real since my pops (R.I.P. Brandywine Slim). Jason truly is the last of a dyin' breed. This man continues to pen classics and don't how to stop. We love you big homie! Never give up!

Aight, aight…I'm done. I release you into Yvonna's world. Watch ya backs and stay low when you readin' this one. You neva know when Gabriella might show up.

Be easy!!

Charisse Washington
VP, The Cartel Publications
www.thecartelpublications.com
www.twitter.com/cartelbooks
www.myspace.com/thecartelpublications
www.facebook.com/cartelcafeandbooks

Prologue
TWENTY SOMETHIN' YEARS EARLIER

The thunderous boom of feet stomping from the ceiling sounded as if it were not stable enough to stand strong. It did little to ease the little girl as she entered through the backdoor of the church. Like a dog roaming around an underprivileged neighborhood, her nose caught whiff of the aroma of the fried chicken exiting the tiny house of worship. The members of the choir were oblivious to what was happening in the basement as they bellowed the verses from the book of gospel Hymns with passion.

Once inside, she hustled to the table, which held a spread of fried chicken, green beans, macaroni and cheese along with a wide selection of pies and cakes, made mostly by the members of the congregation. They were going to convene downstairs the moment service was over to enjoy the meal. Opening a purple Smurf book bag, she looked at the stairwell first to be sure no one was coming.

When she was sure they weren't, and with little time on her side, she piled as much food inside of the bag as possible. It would be food for a few days. And she needed all she could get because her underdeveloped body was malnutritioned and she looked sickly. She could hear the choir's tone softening, indicating service would be over soon. Realizing her bag was stuffed to capacity, she made her way to the door until she heard a powerful deep voice behind her.

"What are you doin' down here, chile?!"

"Nothin'...uh...I was...just," the little girl couldn't get her lies in order.

The man covered in his black, gold and purple preacher's robe walked hurriedly toward her. The child tugged at the door but was no match for a sixty year old man who before being a preacher, worked most of his life as an underpaid construction worker. His endurance was intact.

"You're not goin' nowhere 'til you tell me what ya doin' here." He said hovering over her. He stooped down to scare the truth out of her.

The little girl dropped her head and felt her stomach pound inside her belly. The smells of the food had caused her to experience body pangs all over. She was salivating and wandered how much food she'd be able to swallow, if she took a chance and stuffed as much of it in her mouth as possible.

"I'm hungry." Her soft voice said. "I didn't want to steal. Honest." A single tear escaped her eyes.

"So why would you? From a church of all places? Where are your parents?" The look on the child's face turned to horror. "I bet they don't know what you're doin'. Do they?"

She shook her head over and over. "P...P...Please don't tell on me. I'm hungry. That's all. I won't ever come again."

The preacher's heart softened as he saw the fear in the child's eyes. He wondered what had her so vexed. Scaring her had done nothing but made him feel for her even more. He released the tension from his neck and allowed his shoulders to drop. Standing up straight he said, "Stay right there. Don't you move an inch. You hear me?"

She nodded and he fixed her a large plate. "Come over here." He instructed pointing at a table with two chairs. She did. "Have a seat."

The child dropped her book bag and hustled to the table. Once sitting down, she stuffed her mouth with forkful after forkful. The preacher sat in amazement as he looked at the meal, which was vanishing before his eyes.

"What's your name, girl?"

She held onto the fork tightly but placed no more food inside her chops. Chewing slowly she gazed into the strangers eyes. And at that moment, the preacher felt what was being said without words. She was trying to determine if she could trust him.

Looking at the food before her she slowly said, "Gabriella. My name is Gabriella."

LET THE GAMES BEGIN

The fall wind whipped around Ming's beautiful black Panamera Porsche, the Friday afternoon that Yvonna was released. "What's on mind, Yvonna?" She had just taken her to buy used silver Acura RSX, which was being delivered to Penny's house the next day. "You don't like the car? Ming told you she would buy you another one, but you won't let Ming." Silence. "Well...do you know what you're going to do?" she probed looking over at her plain ponytail and drab blue sweat suit.

Yvonna's wasn't listening to Ming's dumb ass. She was thinking of the advice the doctor gave her upon her release.

'Yvonna, you're going to reach a point where you'll feel you can control your illness. But you should know that there's no controlling schizophrenia. People have tried but failed. But,' she said placing her hand on her shoulder, *'if you feel down, like you don't want to do anything, break the pills in half and take them that way. But always...always...take your medicine. If you don't your mind will convince you of the most absurd things and*

1

you'll find yourself in the craziest of situations.'

"You should let Ming take you to buy some clothes," Ming said not pleased with how basic her friend looked.

"I'll buy my own when I get a job."

"You? A job?" she laughed, her short shiny bob bouncing along with her extreme head movements.

"Yes," Yvonna frowned, although she hadn't worked since her ex-fiancé, Terrell, had rescued her from the office assistant position she held at his doctor's office. "I have to take care of me and Delilah myself."

"You can work for Ming," she said pointing to herself. "No worries."

"Ming, I ain't about to be up in no funky ass nail salon with you. So forget about it." She said rubbing the sweat from her palms onto her pants.

"Don't assume you know all there is to know about Ming. I have more than one job. And funky?" She frowned, "Please!" she said waving her hand in the air. "Nothing funky but that man bitch Penny you moving with."

"Mind your business." Yvonna said rolling her eyes. "Penny cares about me."

"Well Ming don't trust the bitch. You should stay with Ming instead. Ming not been good to you?"

"You heard the doctor," Yvonna said irritated. "I'm being released into Penny's custody for six months. So please stop," she said glancing over at her. "I'm not up for your shit."

Yvonna turned her attention to the Nextel phone the doctor had given her before she left. She assumed Ming brought it for her like she did everything else."

"Do you have the number to this yet?" she asked raising the phone.

"Fuck that phone!" Ming spat.

Yvonna slumped into the butter soft seat and looked

around. Being in the car depressed her a little. Although she always came up on a little cash, she was never able to floss like she wanted to.

"If Ming was black, you'd stay with Ming. But since Ming is not a nigger you won't."

"You sound extremely fuckin' stupid!" Yvonna said rubbing her throbbing temples. "Back in the day I'd yoke your ass up behind that shit you said," she said looking out the window, "but right now, I don't even have the energy."

When she looked over at Ming, she saw tears streaming down her face.

"What's wrong with you, Ming? You've been out of it for the past couple of weeks."

"Ming is alone." She said under her breath. "And Ming's scared."

"Ming, you got twenty aunts and thirty uncles in China alone! So what are you talking about you have no one?"

"Fuck them! They only care about what Ming can do for them. Nothing else!" She was filled with rage and it made Yvonna uncomfortable. "I lost the one person who loved me."

Yvonna didn't know how to react. It was better for her to run from emotion then it was for her to run into it. "Ming, maybe we should chill a little bit."

"Why you say that? Just cause Ming upset you end friendship?"

"I'm not ending our friendship. I just need time to get myself together. My daughter needs me and I need her and right now that's all that matters."

Ming started driving recklessly down the road. She sped in and out of traffic like a Nascar driver and didn't care that her cute 3-year old baby boy named Boy, was in the backseat fast asleep.

Ming whipped her Porsche into the parking spot outside of Penny's house and said, "You here. Get out Ming's car!"

Yvonna looked over at her and said, "I'll call you later."

"Out now!" she screamed waking her beautiful three-year-old son, Boy from his slumber. He palmed his soft brown face until he let out a large cry.

"Okay, Ming." Not wanting to argue, Yvonna grabbed her green army bag and walked up the steps leading to Penny's home. Ming sped off without waiting for her to get inside.

"What the fuck is wrong with her stupid ass?" she said out loud.

Knocking twice, Penny quickly opened the door holding Delilah in her arms. Delilah was not your average child. Her beauty was impressive and her eyes held a lot of mystery. She looked cute in the pink dress Ming bought for her last birthday. "Yvonna, come on in, chile." Penny said opening the door.

Delilah played with the long pink scarf Penny wore around her neck, clueless to Yvonna's presence. "How'd you get here?" Penny questioned looking Yvonna over.

Yvonna caught Penny's investigative stares on the sweat suit she wore. And as far as she was concerned Penny had a nerve when it looked like she was sporting the outfit Cicely Tyson wore in the mini-series, 'Roots'.

"Ming. She just dropped me off." She said pointing at the door.

"I woulda came and got ya, chile. Yous just had to let me know."

"Not a big deal, I'm home now," she said trying to get use to the way *'home'* sounded rolling off her tongue.

Yvonna walked fully inside and noticed that Penny had

purchased brand new furniture throughout the home and she was surprised. All of the old effects were gone and Penny's home finally spoke to modern times. There were flat screen TV's on the wall in the kitchen and living room and two large stylish glove-soft rich brown leather sofas with gold accented arms sat in the middle of the floor.

"Wow! This can't be the same place! You finally came into the future, Penny!" Yvonna said placing her bag down.

"What you tryin' to say? That Penny is old?" She snapped.

Yvonna looked at her surprised at her outburst. "I was giving you a compliment. Are you okay?"

"Oh...yeah...just tired of people judgin' me," she said placing Delilah down who clung at her leg as if Yvonna's presence frightened her. "Yous hungry?"

"Sure," Yvonna said not feeling her response. She stooped down and said, "Come here, baby. Mama's home. I missed you so much."

"Leave her be," Penny interrupted. "She'll come when she's ready."

"But she's my daughter," she said standing up straight, "and I want to build our bond."

"She knows who yous are. Remember...I use to bring her to see you all the time."

"Come here, Delilah." Yvonna challenged.

Delilah didn't move. Instead she clung onto Penny so tightly; it caused discomfort to the bad leg she gained as a result of working so many hours.

Yvonna stood up and tried to push the pain out of her heart her daughter caused. "Well if she don't want to come, she doesn't have to." Yvonna said grabbing her bag from the floor. "I'm tired anyway and I need to get some sleep."

Yvonna moved to the basement door and was about to turn the knob until Penny said, "Don't worry, 'bout nothin', chile." Yvonna felt Penny was happy to be getting rid of her judging by the smile she wore on her face. "I'll take care of her."

"I bet you will."

Yvonna was about to enter the basement until Penny stopped her again. "How do you feel? I mean...how do you *really* feel?"

"What do you mean? Do you wanna know if I'm still seein' people?" Penny nodded. "No. I'm not."

"Good. I'll bring ya food down a little..." her sentence was interrupted when the phone rang. "I wonder if this is the young man who called you earlier."

"A man? Called me?" Yvonna was shocked. She hadn't had a man call her anything in years.

Penny picked up the phone. "Who's callin'?" She paused "What's your name young man?" Penny paused again. "Swoopes," she said outstretching her arm with the handset. "He says his name is Swoopes."

PUSH

"You not gonna stand me up this time are you?" Carmen asked in a voice so seductive, it got Bricks' dick hard. She reminded him of a black Marilyn Monroe.

A smile came to his face when he realized his Jump-Off, the chick he fucked every now and again, would be coming in town from Georgia soon to stay with him for two weeks. Picturing the way Carmen's ass looked like a complete circle when she bent over got him thick with anticipation.

"I ain't stand you up last time," he said as he sat at the light, his eyes fixated on the police car behind him.

"You sure 'bout that? 'Cause I remember me comin' up there only to find out you was out of town."

"Duty called. I had to handle bizness"

"And I called too. Bricks, I don't mind travelin' 'cross states to see you, just as long as there's somethin' at the end of the rainbow when I get there."

"You wild as shit."

"I'm for real. I ain't seen you since the last time you came to the 'A' and I miss you. I ask Kelsi 'bout you all the time but he don't be trying to tell me nothin'. Why are you so elusive?"

"Elusive huh?" he laughed at her use of words. "Ya'll college chicks be killin' me. It ain't like I ain't feelin' you, I just ain't wit' the girlfriend boyfriend thing. I like my space. Feel me?"

She sighed and said, "One day you'll be mine. Because us southern girls can cook, fuck and keep house. So once you get a hold of a southern bell, you should really do your best to keep her."

He laughed and said, "Well, we'll see 'bout all that when you get here. I gotta take care of a situation behind me. I'ma get up wit' you later." He said ending the call.

As he focused on the police car, he knew the moment the light turned green, the cop would be on his trail. He couldn't get caught. He had eight bricks of that White Girl in his trunk and his Godson was in the front strapped in a car seat. He was breaking the law on many levels.

"Aigh't lil, nigga, if we get out of this," he said to his Godson, "I'ma put a lil somethin' in that bottle to make you nice for the rest of the night.

The 24-month old baby, whom everyone called Chomps, smiled, gripped his brown chunky foot, and jammed it in his mouth. Bricks smiled at him and the moment the light turned green, he pulled his 2006 Dodge Challenger into traffic, and like clockwork, the cop turned on his sirens.

"Bitch ass nigga," Bricks said pressing heavily on the gas pedal. "Too fuckin' predictable."

Bricks handled the roads and even stopped seconds from hitting a white work van by dipping quickly to the right, but the cop was still on him. So he sped faster missing an old lady pushing a cart full of junk. Still...the Bladensburg police officer could not be shook. He wanted

Bricks badly knowing that whatever caused him to elude him in the first place, would be a big payoff at the station.

Bricks pushed the limits of his car and was determined that the racist Bladensburg police officer would not catch him. So when he came to another light, and couldn't get through the cars waiting, he drove up on the curb and back on the street again. He couldn't lie, he was having fun. Chomps was thrown around in his seat a little but for the most part, was safe, laughing and enjoying the ride. Soon Bricks grew tired of the games.

"Fuck!" he yelled slamming his hand on the steering wheel, looking through his rear view mirror at the red, white and blue flashing lights.

Passing the Peace Cross in Bladensburg Maryland, his heart dropped when he saw the crossing posts come down indicating a train was on its way. If this happened, his path would be blocked and he would no doubt be arrested, unless he got into a shoot out with the officer. If the baby wasn't with him, he may have taken the chance.

Placing his hand on the baby's chest to prevent him from falling out of his seat, he gripped the steering wheel tightly and mashed the tip of his foot on the gas pedal. His butter colored Timberland boot creased so deeply, it looked as if it would break in half. While the other cars stopped and waited for the train to pass, he drove past the flashing stop sign, through the white wooden guardrail, and halfway over the tracks but the wheels got hung up on the tracks. He gave it some gas but all it did was disturb the gravel beneath his tires. Onlookers grabbed their mouths in fear.

"Stupid, fool!" The cop yelled safely on the right side of the tracks. "You're not worth my life."

Bricks didn't care about imminent danger he was concerned about being arrested. The front tires made it safely across but the back tires still had not. The train was only a few feet from ripping the car in half so he pressed the gas a little more and looked at the train coming at him full speed on the right.

"God, I got this kid in the car! You gotta let me have this one."

He gave it some more gas and this time the car lifted off the railing. He was released! But the second his back tires moved off the track, the side of the train scraped at his bumper, spinning the car in a wild spiral motion into the street. Not trying to lose total control, he didn't jam the brakes and instead, hoped for a safe stop. It's exactly what he got. When he finally came to a halt, he hit the gas and sped from the scene. His breaths were heavy and when he looked over at Chomps, he was smiling with his cell-phone in his mouth.

"When the fuck you get that, lil nigga?" He joked. The baby cooed and the cell phone rang.

When he answered it he couldn't believe who was on the line. Last time he hung out with her, she held a lot of mystery and that made him uncomfortable. In his line of work people had to be on the up and up at all times. In fact, his brother Melvin said she was a hustler's nightmare and shouldn't be trusted and he knew he was right. But...there was something about her that appealed to him. *Fuck it.* He thought to himself. *I got some time to spare. I mean, how bad could she really be?*

UNEXPECTED COMPANY

"Bricks, it's Yvonna. Can...can I see you?" Yvonna knew she hadn't spoken to him in a while, but for whatever reason, his number was the only one she remembered.

"Man, I ain't heard from you in years, now you callin' me? Fuck you want?"

"I've been away. And I really wanna see you, if you're not busy."

Bricks looked over at Chomps who was smiling with his other foot in his mouth and said, "Where you at?"

"I'm in Mount Rainer, Maryland. 4255 34th Street."

"Gimme a hour. I gotta drop this chick off at my cousin's house," he said referring to the coke in his trunk, "and get my other car. I'll scoop you up then."

"Thank you, Bricks. I appreciate this." Yvonna brushed her hair with her hand into a neater ponytail as she stood outside of Penny's crib anxiously waiting.

Swoopes' call frightened her and her mind wandered to their conversation.

"Yvonna...you're home." Swoopes said calmly. "You

don't know how long I've been waitin' for this day, shawty."

"Swoopes...how...how did you get Penny's number?"

"It's ways to get in touch with anybody. You should know that more than anyone."

"Look...I'm sorry for whatever I may have done to you. I really am, but I'm changed now. I'm not the same person."

"Changed?" he laughed. "You and change? Naw...I like the old Yvonna better. I got some shit to handle with her. Where she at?"

"Swoopes, look, I forgive you for the things you did to me, and you have to forgive me for whatever I did to you. I mean...all's fair in war. I'ma mother now, and all I want to do is move on with my life and take care of my baby."

"Fuck I care 'bout that kid just cause you pushed it out that funky pussy of yours. You'll see me. And you'll see me real soon too. Be ready."

Yvonna shivered because out of everyone she had wronged, she knew he was the most dangerous. The conversation was still going through her mind until she heard loud banging music. The rapper Drake's voice moved closer and closer to where she stood until she could hear his lyrics clearly.

"You comin' or not?" Bricks asked through his rolled down passenger window. Yvonna hurried to the silver Hummer and stopped short when she saw a baby in the front seat. "Get in the back," he instructed her.

She had to admit, Bricks looked better than she remembered and she was stuck. He covered his grey eyes with a pair of smoked out black glasses, which sat against his chestnut colored skin. And his husky build filled out the black Christian Audigier sweatshirt he wore with ease.

"You aight?" he asked when she continued to stare at him.

"Oh...uh...yeah. I'm fine." She still hadn't gotten into the car.

"Well get in the back." He said as he tugged at his ear, which held a 6-carat diamond earring. She hustled in the backseat and they drove a few blocks before he finally cut the music down and spoke to her. "What you want man?"

"I wanted to see you." She smiled looking at him intently.

"Stop playin' games, shawty. That's why I neva really fucked wit' you cause you always got other motives."

"I'm serious, Bricks. I was just lookin' to get out the house and you were the first person I thought of."

"You ain't tryin' to fuck so what you want?"

"Bricks, why does everything have to be about that with you? You don't have no friends you just hang out with?"

"Yeah, and I got enough of them."

She couldn't tell him that she was afraid to stay at Penny's because if Swoopes found her number, she knew he knew where she lived too. "Well maybe I can change your mind," she said, softly. Glancing at the baby she said," That's your son?"

"No. He's my Godson."

"He's cute. What's his name?"

"Chomps." He said spinning the steering wheel to the right, his diamond Cartier watch glistening under the fall sunlight.

"Chomps? Someone named a baby Chomps?"

"Yeah. It's his nickname."

"Why?"

"Cause he always got somethin' in his mouth. But fuck all that, you tryin' to get a room or what?"

Yvonna exhaled and said, "No."

"Then what's up? 'Cause I'm five seconds from dropping you back off."

"You wanna get somethin' to eat?" she offered although she was dead broke.

"You treatin'?" he asked trying to push her buttons. He hated that she never said much about anything but it was the same thing he liked about her.

"I don't have any money, Bricks I'm just tryin' to think of somethin' we can do."

"I suggested that already, we can get a room. You tryin' to go or what?"

With nothing else to do she said, "Yeah. We can go."

He had won but he didn't want it that way. He really wanted to find out who she was. "Man quit bullshittin'! You ain't really tryin' to get the room are you?"

"Do I have a choice?"

"I'm just fuckin' wit' you 'bout that shit. I do wanna know what's really up though. I ain't gotta make a bitch do nothin' she don't wanna."

Yvonna looked at Brick's sexy face in the rearview mirror and said, "I just need to get away. Can that be enough?"

He waved to let a car get over in front of him. "Well look, I got some shit to get into later, but maybe I'll take you to grab somethin' to eat first. Cool?"

"Cool," she smiled.

The moment they agreed, a black Ford Crown Victoria pulled up on the left of the truck and then another pulled up on the right. Finally a third pulled up to the back, and in sync, they rolled their windows down and fired into Brick's Hummer.

"What the fuck!" He said as he ducked down and mashed on his gas pedal for the second time that day. Raising his shirt, he removed his 9 milli from his waist, and fired out of the shattered window, over the baby's head on his right. The shooters wouldn't stop and they continued to unload bullets into his vehicle shattering the glass to pieces.

"Can you shoot?!" He yelled to Yvonna who was ducking in the back seat.

"W...what?"

"I said can you fuckin' shoot? Wake the fuck up! Niggas is tryin' to kill us!"

"Y...yes. I can." She nodded still stooped down. "I'm scared."

"Fuck bein' scared. I'ma need you to prove to me you can blast," he said tossing another 9 from his console at Yvonna. "Buck them mothafucka's!"

Although frightened, and trying her best not to relive her violent past, she stuck her head out of the broken glass window and started firing at the shooters behind her. Her aim was so accurate, that she managed to hit the driver in his shoulder, causing the car to spiral into another car on the road. Because of her skills, they now had only two cars to deal with.

Bricks, while controlling the steering wheel, was now shooting out of the shattered window on the left. He looked over frequently to be sure the baby was okay. And although Chomps wasn't hurt, he was no longer putting things into his mouth like he normally did. He was scared and crying at the top of his lungs. Shards of glass covered his soft black curly hair and that angered Bricks. He cared about the kid and hated putting him in danger for the second time that day. But another gunshot flew into the right side of the truck ripping into Brick's arm.

"Ahhhhhhhh!" he screamed out.

The Hummer swerved wildly before he got it under control with one hand. But he could no longer keep them off of their trail. It had to be Yvonna who was going to take them out. He only had one good arm available and he needed it to drive.

Yvonna kicked the broken glass out of the back right window and fired hitting the driver in his head. The Ford coiled a few times before hitting a light post. But it was two down and one to go. But Bricks no longer feeling up for the bullshit decided to pull off of the main road, and onto a residential street to wait for the third car to pull up. He took his jacket off, placed it on the floor and lifted the baby out the car seat and placed him on top of the jacket, shaking some of the glass out of his hair. He was trying to protect Chomps from a stray bullet as best he could, given the situation. The street was quiet with the exception of Chomps cries within the bullet-ridden truck, which looked extremely out of place on the block.

"What you doing? They gonna kill us!" Yvonna asked breathing heavily looking all around her.

"Chill out!" he yelled reloading his weapon. His arm was in pain but he kept it together. "I ain't running from these niggas no more. I got this shit."

"Oh my God! Somebody's pullin' up on us." Yvonna said seeing the car creeping up to them on the right.

Bricks held his weapon in his hand, extended it out of the window and was about to fire. But when the driver in the last Ford Victoria got closer, he smiled at them and pulled off. Bricks exhaled.

"What the fuck you know 'bout that shit?!" he yelled at Yvonna, holding his bleeding arm.

Yvonna still coming off of the emotional roller coaster said, "What?! You…you blaming me for this shit?"

"You said you needed to get away, and some niggas just shot up my truck! Fuck yeah I'm blamin' you!" He said lifting the baby off the floor and placing him back into the car seat. "And how the fuck you know how to shoot?"

"I just do," she said in a low voice.

"What the fuck you got me caught up in, shawty?"

"You a fuckin' drug dealer whose name is Bricks," she said finding blame with the mention of his name. "It seems natural that you'd have someone trying to kill you."

"First of all nobody is crazy enough to fuck wit' me. And half of the niggas in Maryland and DC know my name. I ain't neva had some shit like that go down unless I started it."

"So just cause you think you tough, you think you untouchable too?"

"Like I said, ain't nobody been crazy enough to fuck wit' me 'til now."

"You ridin' around the city with a baby who ain't even yours, Bricks. How tough can you possibly be?"

"Yvonna, you got five minutes to tell me who them niggas were." He said turning around with the gun in his hand. "I'm not askin' you no more, I'm tellin' you."

He took off his glasses and his grey eyes pierced through Yvonna. She exhaled realizing she was in over her head. She knew the dudes were members of Swoopes' crew, the YBM (Young Black Millionaires). She recognized his cousin Cane, as the one who had just pulled up and pulled off. But she also knew if she got too excited, that there was a risk of Gabriella showing up. And as far as she was concerned, the only one any of them had to worry about was that bitch. If Yvonna told Bricks who was involved, a war would ensue and when the smoke cleared, they'd all be aiming at her.

"I'm sorry, Bricks, but I don't know anything about this. I'll find a way home."

Brushing the broken glass fragments off of her body,

17

she exited the truck and ran away. Bricks made a vow that no matter what, he'd never fuck with that bitch again, and he had all intentions on keeping that promise.

ADDICTED

When Ming scooped Yvonna up and took her to her house, she was thrown off by her beautiful castle style home at Woodmore South in Mitcheville Maryland. Once inside Ming said, "You go to living room. Ming, will make you something to eat."

Yvonna walked slowly into the elaborately furnished house while Ming rushed upstairs to do something that was obviously so important, it caused her to drop her Louis Vuitton purse in the center of her plush pink carpeted floor. Minutes later she came downstairs ran to the kitchen and grabbed some ingredients to make some stir-fried rice with steak. Yvonna followed her into the kitchen and took a seat on the barstool.

"Had something to take care of upstairs?" Yvonna inquired.

"Yes, Ming's boyfriend upstairs."

Yvonna raised her eyebrows, giggled and said, "*Boyfriend?* When did that happen?"

"Can't remember." She shrugged. "But he fucks well

and he likes the way Ming sucks his dick." Yvonna laughed. "Seriously, Ming takes the entire thing down her throat. What were you doing away from home?" She skipped the subject. "I thought you wanted to spend time with Delilah."

"I changed my mind." Yvonna said not able to get over the dick in throat thing. "Where's, Boy?"

"He's over my aunt's house. We going back to China soon and Boy go with me."

"Your ass stay in China."

"It's home."

"I wish I had a home," Yvonna said softly.

"You want drink? You look like things are heavy on mind."

"Yeah. Give me some Ciroc straight up." Ming paused what she was doing, got the liquor and returned to the food.

"Drink up. It'll make you feel nice."

Yvonna allowed the warm liquor to enter her body. She was trying her best not to allow Swoopes and the way her only child treated her earlier, to affect the rest of her day. She was also trying to be a normal member of society...but after the shoot out, she didn't know if that was possible. Ming dished up the food and placed a plate in front of Yvonna before she took one upstairs and returned empty handed.

"You wanna fuck?" Ming asked dishing up another plate for herself. She sat at the bar in the kitchen. Her feet dangled underneath her small body. "My boyfriend wants to fuck you."

Yvonna coughed. "You're kidding right?"

"Don't act like you haven't fucked Ming before."

"Well I *don't* want to fuck Ming now."

Ming frowned and when Yvonna looked by the stairwell, a fine ass black man favoring the actor Lance Gross appeared holding an empty plate in his hand. His dark chocolate skin caught the golden shine of the chandelier and made Yvonna reconsider her decision of not having a little fun with him.

"Baby, I'm out," he said to Ming although he looked at Yvonna. "The food was great."

Ming kissed him passionately and groped his penis. Yvonna knew the show was for her but she liked it. "Ming will call you later," she said looking up at him.

He squeezed her nipple, looked at Yvonna again and said, "I *better* hear from ya soon." Yvonna felt the demand was directed at her and she felt uncomfortable.

When he left Yvonna said, "You betta watch out for that one. He might get away."

"Naw, Ming has him. He works for me sometimes too. We do business and pleasure very well together."

Yvonna rolled her eyes and said, "That man works in a nail salon, Ming?"

"Ming told you she has more than one job. I'll leave it at that."

While Ming picked at her food, Yvonna's phone rang. It was Bricks.

"Aye, Yvonna, where you at?" he said in a mellow but serious tone. "I gotta talk to you. And I gotta talk to you now."

"Well I'm busy, Bricks." She looked at Ming who was eavesdropping.

"Bitch, I don't give a fuck. Either get at me tonight, or I'm bringin' this heat to your doorstep. What you wanna do?"

Not wanting him blowing up the spot in front of Penny's house she said, "Give me your address and I'll be on my way."

All The Way In It

15 MINUTES EARLIER

After getting the bullet removed at the hospital by some broad he fucked from time to time, he was on his way to his house in Landover Maryland. The moment he turned on 65th avenue, he waved at his seven year old cousin Tracy who lived in the first house on the block. The little girl with two long pigtails, wearing a purple dress, played happily alone with her doll.

"What you doin' out here? It's gettin' dark."

"The ice cream truck 'bout to come. Can I have five dollars cousin, Bricks?"

He reached in his pocket, handed her the bill and said,

"Where your mother at?" He gripped his arm when he felt a sharp pain shoot through it.

"She over aunt Shelby's house."

Bricks shook his head in disgust. Her mother had been with his cousin for ten years and she was as worthless of a mother as they came. But his cousin Jace was so sick in love, that he couldn't see past her green eyes, thick ass and wet pussy.

"Look...after the truck comes, go in the house. If I see you outside when I roll back up the block, I'ma fuck your lil' young ass up. Hear me?"

"Yes, cousin Bricks." She laughed not disturbed by her cousin's threats.

He pulled off and waved at his cousins on the block, most of which were men. Most of his family lived on that street and they were deep. The set-up started for business purposes, they were all involved in the drug business together. But soon it just became the family way.

They were all doing regular shit like washing their cars, sitting on the steps of their house shooting craps, when he pulled up to his house. Bricks pulled behind his bullet riddled Hummer and shook his head. He loved that truck and he hated that it was all fucked up...but what could he do?

Bricks jumped out of the car, grabbed the kid from his car seat and was preparing to walk inside the house when someone called his name. "Bricks. Let me rap to you for a second."

Before he turned around, he could tell by the sound of the stranger's voice that something wasn't right. Slowly he pivoted, with the child in his arm.

"Open the door," he yelled at the house. His eyes remained on the driver. "Somebody come get Chomps!"

"Boy, why you yellin' and shit?" Kendal asked, swinging the door open before seeing the stranger.

"What's up, ma?" the stranger said to her. "You lookin' mighty sexy today."

"Get the fuck in the house, Kendal."

Realizing the all black Dodge Magnum with black tinted windows meant trouble; she grabbed Chomps and ran into the house. When he was safe, he slowly walked down his steps, stopping a few feet from the car. He placed his hand on his waist, validating that his heat was in place. The stranger looked like the rapper Fabolous, and his chocolate skin and mellow mannerisms made them even more alike. Bricks took notice that all of the windows were rolled up except the one on the passenger side. *Are more niggas in the car?* He thought.

"I know you're probably wondering who I am," he said wiping his chin with his mutilated hand, which was missing two fingers. "I would wonder too if I were you," he smiled.

"Only thing I'm wonderin' is what the fuck you must be on to roll up on my block." He gritted.

"I come in peace."

"Nigga, I ain't got time for that shit. What the fuck you want, son? 'Cause you ain't said shit." Bricks said trying to bypass the pain in his shoulder.

"We have a mutual acquaintance that has a knack for stirrin' up shit, and gettin' niggas involved in wars. I suggest you stay the fuck away from her."

"You threatin' me?" He asked taking one step closer to the car. Bricks didn't handle threats well.

"I don't know you to threaten you. I'm sayin' stay the fuck away from Yvonna. Me and her got unfinished business. Now I'm sorry you had to get caught up in the cross fire today," he said nodding at Brick's truck, "but you truly gotta mind the company you keep."

Bricks was heated but he wanted to know what else he knew about him before he made his next move. "How you know where I live?" He asked through clenched teeth.

"I know everything 'bout you, nigga. And you know nothin' about me. So like I said, stay the fuck away from that bitch. I got plans for her and I don't want nobody standing in my way. I'm doin' you a favor by comin' here."

"Whoever the fuck I keep time wit' is my business, nigga!"

"You've been warned," he paused. "And by the way, the name's Swoopes."

"Swoopes, huh?" he nodded biting his bottom lip so hard it almost bled. "Well Swoopes, you got otha shit to worry 'bout now."

"Like what?"

"Like how you gonna get outta here alive."

When Swoopes looked around, every nigga that was doing regular shit on the block had suddenly surrounded his car and had their weapons aimed in his direction. Bricks didn't have to alert his family, the outsider rolling up on the block was enough to bring them together. That type of thing never happened.

Swoopes wiped his chin with his hand again, looked at the ten birds aiming at his car and said, "I see it's time for me to go, but we gonna get up again."

"You ain't hearin' me, slim." Bricks pulled out his gun and aimed at him. "Get the fuck out of the car before we light that mothafucka up!"

"Naw, nigga!" he said raising his voice for the first time. "You ain't hearin' me," he rolled his back window down, revealing another man in the back, with his little cousin Tracy sitting on his lap. Only Bricks could see his cousin because the other windows remained closed. "We'll get together next time."

Bricks couldn't believe Tracy got in the car when she knew better. And there she was, eating ice cream and sitting on the stranger's lap like he was Santa Claus.

"You aight, Tracy?" he asked keeping his eyes on Swoopes.

"Yeah. The nice man bought me some ice cream."

"That's cool," he said motioning for his cousins to lower their weapons. But they hesitated, confused at hearing Tracy's name. "But didn't I tell you to go in the house earlier?

"He's real nice, cousin Bricks."

"Fuck that nigga, Tracy," he said biting his bottom lip again. "So what you gonna do wit' my peoples?" He asked Swoopes when their weapons went down.

"I'ma drop her off up the block, now if you follow me, I'ma put a big ass whole in that lil bitty face of hers. Got me?"

"I'm scared, cousin Bricks." She said hearing the threat.

"Everything gonna be cool, Tracy. Okay?"

"Yes," she said wiping her tears. Finally she realized the danger she was in.

Bricks smiled and eyed Swoopes. "Slim, all that ain't even necessary."

"We'll see. Just remember what I said...stay the fuck away from them folks. Unless you want this kind of shit on your block all the time."

Bricks didn't want to tell him that he was straight tripping if he thought he could make it on or off his block alive ever again.

Swoopes drove off and his cousins and him all piled into the middle of the street. When the car was further down the block, Bricks waited anxiously. A minute later, Tracy came running up the street and he was able to breathe. "Yo, who the fuck was that?" Forty, Brick's oldest cousin asked.

"I don't know, but I'm 'bout to find out." He grabbed his phone and reconnected with the person Swoopes warned him to stay away from.

LADY STRIFE

The moment Ming bent the corner and turned onto Brick's block, for some reason, Yvonna could sense that Swoopes had been there. Strangers she didn't know grimaced at them as they hugged the corner leading to Brick's house. It looked like everyone was on guard from something.

"Where ya'll goin'?" one of the men asked when they were halfway up the block.

"We goin' to see, Bricks," Yvonna said shocked at being stopped.

"Hold up," the man said as he reached in his phone for his cell. Seconds later, having gotten the approval from Bricks, he said, "Go 'head."

"That was crazy," Yvonna said looking back at the man. "I wonder what that was about."

Ming parked her car and said, "I don't know but I'm goin' with you." She grabbed her crocodile hobo purse. "So don't even try to leave me out here with them." She said looking around.

"Ya'll Chinese always scared of niggas."

"Ming not the only one scared. Look at you."

"Who is it?" a high pitch female voice asked at the door.

"Yvonna," she said looking at Ming with a perplexed glare. She couldn't believe he invited her over the house with a girl there. She wasn't considering that their visit was strictly business. "You think that's his girlfriend?"

Ming shrugged her shoulders and picked at the non-existent dirt specs under her nails before looking back at the men who were eyeing them.

Kendal Blake, who was beautiful, opened the door and they were eager to walk inside, because the men's stares made them uncomfortable. But the moment they moved inward, Kendal pushed them back outside.

"I ain't say ya'll could come in," she yelled rolling her eyes. Her sepia colored skin turned a shade red. "Wait out there," Kendal continued, leaving the door partially open.

"Ming guess that's how she got that gash on her forehead. She don't know how to talk to people."

The golden lounge dress she wore flopped on the couch and it did nothing to conceal her voluptuous shape. She was a knock out, hands down.

"Why the fuck you leave her out there?" Bricks asked, approaching the door. He hadn't bothered to acknowledge Yvonna. "I told you to let her in when she gets here."

"I left her out there, 'cause she the reason all this shit happened!"

"Bitch, this my house! If I tell you to do something, do it!"

Kendal, angry, clasped the cordless phone that sat in her lap and threw it at him. The hard plastic handset landed on his forehead and lacerated his skin. He lunged in her direction but she ran into her bedroom slamming the door. Bricks kicked the door with extreme force and followed it up with a closed fist. Still, the wooden door wouldn't budge.

"I want you out of my mothafuckin' house tomorrow, nigga!" He spat pointing at the door as if she stood before him. "I'm sick of this shit!"

"Fuck you, bitch! I ain't goin nowhere!"

"Come in," Bricks said wiping the blood from his forehead, locking the door behind them. His face wore a mean frown.

When they walked deeper into the living room, they saw piles of neatly folded clothes against the wall and two gathered cots on the right of the television. With all of the items in the living room, things were still neat.

"Go downstairs," he instructed, pointing at a door on the opposite end of the one Kendal ran into. "And who the fuck is this?" He questioned looking at Ming.

"My ride."

"I said I was taking you home."

"Well I don't trust you," she said walking down the steps leading to another door.

"Hold up, let me unlock that."

He walked in front of them, used his key and turned the knob. When the door opened they couldn't believe how fly everything was. A large flat screen TV hung on the wall, with the surround system below it. Two beautiful green sofas sat in the middle of the floor and a large table sat in the far right with track lighting above it.

Bricks locked the door behind them and said, "Sit down." They sat on the couch and he grabbed a hard metal chair and sat across the table from them. Yvonna could tell he was trying to calm down after the fight upstairs. "Ya'll smoke?"

"What's up Bricks?" Yvonna questioned getting to the point. She moved a little in her seat worried at his response.

He grabbed a cigar box from under the glass table, removed a blunt, and said, "What the fuck is a Swoopes?"

Yvonna sunk into the body of the sofa and sighed. She thought about lying but both Ming and Bricks were staring so far in her mouth, she felt they could see her ovaries.

"You not going to let this go are you?" she asked as Ming accepted the blunt handoff from Bricks. She wished she wasn't so eager to accept his gesture but saying something to Ming was like talking to her asshole. It's gonna do what it's gonna do.

"Who the fuck is Swoopes?" He asked again releasing smoke into the air.

"He's somebody who has a beef with me and he's trying to kill me. I'm sorry if you all up in this now, but you should know it's not what I wanted."

"Bitch, you hear yourself?" he asked scooting closer to the table, emptying the ashes onto a beautiful cherry-wood ashtray. "You tellin' me this shit afta the fact?"

"It all happened so quickly."

"Why the fuck you ain't tell me you had a hit on your head? I had you all up in my car and shit!" He dropped the blunt and Ming picked it up and sucked on it like it was loaded dick. Yvonna looked at her and shook her head.

"You really should calm the fuck down," she told Ming under her breath. "You actin' jive extra." Ming waved her off. Turning her attention to Bricks she said, "He only shot at you because I was with you, you'll probably never see him again."

"The nigga showed his face on my block...today." Yvonna felt hate radiate from him and she wished she never came.

"He...he has it in his mind that I had something to do with him getting locked up. But he did a lot of shit to me and had whatever happened to him coming."

"Where he live?" Bricks asked not feeling up for the ceremonies anymore. He wanted both of them bitches out of his crib.

"I don't know. He could be anywhere in Maryland or DC. We knew the same people and at one point ran in the same circle but I haven't seen him in years."

"I was hopin' to deal wit' this shit tonight," he said standing up. He removed a beer from the small fridge and gulped it down. They looked at him as if he was going to offer them a drink. "I would ask ya'll if ya'll want one, but fuck it." Ming and Yvonna looked at each other. "Tell me what you *do* know about him."

"Bricks, I'm not doing this. This why I ain't wanna say nothing because I knew shit would kick off," she said softly.

Bricks looked at Ming, back and Yvonna and said, "Shawty you need to start talkin' we beyond shit kickin' off! This man came over here and threatened my life and my family and I don't take that shit lightly, I ain't to be fucked wit'!"

Yvonna stood up and said, "Let me go home and think about it."

Bricks walked toward her. "See that won't work," he said putting his hand on her shoulder. "Sit the fuck down." When she didn't he said, "I'm not gonna ask you again." Yvonna begrudgingly sat down. "The nigga told me to stay away from you. If I let you out of my sight, and he deads your ass, I might not be able to find him. I can't have that happen." He was saying one thing but for some reason, Yvonna felt he was worried about her too.

Yvonna looked away from him. "I'm tellin' you it won't stop that easily."

"This nigga SHOT me...showed up at MY HOUSE...and THREATENED my family's safety!" He growled. The veins in his head and arms bulged from his skin. "So until I get him, you stayin' right here wit' me!" He said pointing at the floor.

Ming thinking the situation was sexy, stood up and said, "You want me to pick up anything from Bitch's house? It don't seem like you goin' anywhere no time soon."

Yvonna looked at Bricks and saw the revenge he desired in his sexy grey eyes. She knew she wasn't leaving anytime soon either.

"First off, Ming, it's *the bitch's* house. Not bitch's house. Second of all, bring me some clothes and my medicine." She said looking at Bricks hoping he wouldn't ask what the drugs were for. "And tell Penny I'll call her when I can."

Ming grabbed her purse. "Have fun! Lots of fuck...I mean...fun," she continued trotting up the stairs. "And if you need some help, call me. I'll see you later. "

Yvonna was thoroughly embarrassed by her horniness. Her sex drive lasted longer than a flight from there to Africa.

"So now what?" she asked him when they were alone. "Since you holding me against my will."

"Get some sleep and tomorrow we try and find him."

"Where you sleeping?"

"Upstairs. There's some food in the fridge over there. You can eat if you want, if not, fuck it too. Just don't try and leave. And I think Bet put some clean sheets in the closet over there."

"Who's Bet?"

"Nobody you need to worry about."

Bricks was about to walk up the steps when she was compelled to ask, "Will your girlfriend be mad that I'm here?"

His lips turned down and pierced closely together. "That bitch ain't my girlfriend." he paused. "I'ma lock the door. The quicker this shit is over wit' the better for everybody."

She couldn't agree more so the moment she was alone, she drifted into a deep sleep.

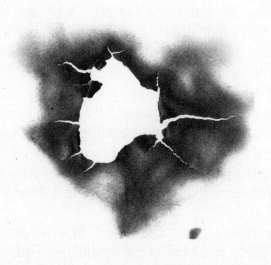

WHEN THE PAST COMES BACK TO HAUNT

Jona sat on her bed looking at the bathroom door. She knew the man inside wasn't the same and she had a feeling she knew why. He was still in love with Yvonna. She walked to the door wondering if she should talk to him or not.

"Terrell, is everything okay?" Jona asked, as she gripped the strings of her red satin robe with one hand, and placed her hand on the door with the other. "I'm worried about you." She touched the fibers of the wood wishing she could touch her man instead.

"I'm fine, Jona!" he yelled causing her to back away. "I told you that when you asked me before." He bolted out the door visibly irritated. "I just have a lot on my mind."

"Do you love me anymore?"

"I don't want to talk about this."

"But I wanna be here for you. We've been together

for years and you still treat me like I'm a stranger." She walked behind him but was sure to maintain her distance. Terrell looked at her, pushed past her again and grabbed his car keys.

"Look at you," he spat. "Nothing about you turns me on. You're dry in the bedroom and your body stinks. I just can't take this anymore. I want out!"

"What?" She sobbed holding her stomach. "Why would you talk to me like that? It doesn't even sound like you anymore."

"I'll be home for dinner."

"Terrell, talk to me." She pleaded. When he didn't answer she said, "Does this have anything to do with Yvonna being home? Do you want to leave me for someone who's fuckin' crazy? Is that what you want?"

"After everything I said, you still hear what you want." He spat. "Fuck dinner, I'll grab something to eat while I'm out."

He hurriedly walked out of their room, and out the front door.

"What's going on with you?" she said to herself. "Where's the man I fell in love with?"

He was gone.

A WOMAN SCORNED

Yvonna was awaken by Penny's call while lying comfortably under a quilt on the couch. She adjusted a little and answered. "Yes."

"Yvonna...is everythin' okay? That Ming girl came by to get ya clothes and your medicine. But where are yous?"

"I just need to take care of some things. I'll be home in a few days."

"O...Okay. Well how ya feel?"

"I'm not having hallucinations anymore so stop worrying."

"Okay...did you take the Clozaril and Lithium?"

Yvonna sighed and said, "Not yet." She paused for a moment when she heard someone walking down the stairs. "Look, I have to go. I'll call when I can."

"Okay, but just so yous know, I don't allow runnin' in and out of my house."

Yvonna looked at the phone and said, "You know what, I don't wanna say something wrong so I'll call you later." She couldn't believe she was acting all funky just because she was staying out a few nights.

Irritated, she threw the covers off her body. Brick's Bladensburg High School Sweatshirt covered her chest and she had nothing but her white cotton panties on below. The moment she saw Kendal standing before her with a pot full of hot grits, her heart raced. Bricks said he'd lock the door so how did she get downstairs? Yvonna jumped back several feet into a corner, her long hair disheveled and all over her head.

"Ain't this somethin'?" Kendal said, eyeing her up and down. "Some bitches just don't know when to stay away."

"What you doin' down here?" Yvonna questioned looking around for an escape, the steam from the grits oozing out of the pot.

"I'm askin' the fuckin' questions!" she said walking closer. "What the fuck you doin' in my house?"

Before Yvonna could answer, she saw a shadow in her peripheral vision on her left. Her heart pumped rapidly and she hesitated before looking. Could it be Gabriella? Turning her head slowly, she was relieved when she didn't see her.

"Look, I'm not trying to cause any problems. I'm just—"

Yvonna's statement was cut short when the girl threw the hot grits on her body burning her chin and legs. The pain felt as if a thousand needles were being stuck into her skin. "Awwwwww!" She screamed wiping the grits off, hopping around the basement. "What is wrong with you?!"

"Fuck that shit! You got me fucked up if you think you gonna be down here shacking up with my man! I'ma kick your fuckin' ass today!" She dropped the pan and took two steps closer to her.

"Look," Yvonna said outstretching her arms, "It's not

even like that between Bricks and me. It's business and that's it."

"Bitch, you don't know who you fuckin' wit'," Kendal bragged. "If you did, you wouldn't be here. Nobody fuck's with me and gets away wit' it."

"Listen, I'm trying not to hurt you. Bricks wants me to help him deal with that situation that happened yesterday and after that, I'll be gone." The pain from the burns still stinging her body.

"*You* hurt *me*?" She laughed. "Neva that!"

Again Yvonna saw the shadow and she knew immediately what was happening. Gabriella was trying to appear and she knew if that happened, Kendal's life would be in danger. Instead of beating her ass like the old Yvonna would have, she ran to the table and twisted off the tops to her pill bottles, tossed a few in her mouth, swallowing them without water. The bottles dropped out of her hands and her entire body trembled.

Kendal couldn't believe her eyes. She was geared up for a fight and didn't get one. Instead Kendal picked up the pill bottles and made mental notes of the medications. *What the fuck is Clozaril and Lithium?* She thought to herself.

"Fuck you doin' down here?" Bricks asked entering the basement.

Kendal turned to look at him and then back at Yvonna and dropped the bottles on the floor. The pills spilled everywhere.

"No! What the fuck is she doin' here?" She asked pointing at her.

Bricks looked at the grits all over Yvonna's clothes and gripped Kendal by the back of her shirt, slamming her into a wall. He had been in pain all night from the gunshot wound to his arm and wasn't up for her bullshit.

"Bitch, what the fuck you doin' down here?"

"Why is she here, Bricks? Why are you doin' this to me?"

"Kendal I swear on everything, if you don't leave out of my basement, I'ma drop you. By the end of the week, I want all your shit out of my house." Kendal looked at him with saddened eyes before her face-hardened.

"I'ma give you some time to cool off. But I'll be back and she better not be here when I do."

"Bitch take your stupid ass up the steps!" He demanded.

Kendal stormed up the stairs. "You aight?" he asked Yvonna.

"Yeah...I'm fine. I guess." She shrugged. "How did she get down here, I thought the door was locked? She got a key?"

"Naw. I must've left the door unlocked by mistake."

"Well what's up with her?"

"Kendal just being Kendal. She delusional and there's more shit goin' on wit' her than you know about. My bad for the shit she did to you though." Yvonna got on her hands and knees and placed her pills back in the bottle. And then she sat on the couch and tugged at his sweatshirt to cover her panties. "What I wanna know is, why you ain't defend yourself? I remember you use to cuss me out all the time."

"Bricks, I'm not like that no more." She sighed. "And I don't wanna be. All I wanna do is take care of my daughter."

Bricks exhaled and said, "It's your funeral. But look...put some clothes on. We gotta roll. I wanna find this dude like yesterday."

"Where we goin'?"

"We gotta stop by Mom's place."

"Your mother is involved?"

"Naw...this nigga name Moms." When she looked at him with a confused stare he said, "It's a long story. But put your shit on so we can go."

THERE'S NO PLACE
LIKE MOM'S

The sky was ice blue and the fiery sun was partially hidden behind large feathery clouds. Immense oak trees surrounded Mom's luxurious mansion, which was located in a quiet suburb in Maryland while Bricks and Yvonna waited patiently at his front door.

"Who is it?" a female voice called.

"Bricks. I'm here to see Moms."

A beautiful white female with long blonde hair swung the door open and smiled at him. She batted her lashes and looked him up and down flirtatiously.

"What's up, Samantha?" He winked.

"You," she said opening the door, frowning at Yvonna. "I guess you have a lot going on though."

"Not what you think," he said once inside. "Where Moms?"

"In the living room. He's waiting on you."

Bricks walked in with Yvonna close on his heels.

There wasn't much furniture throughout the house and when they came to a cherry wood door with brass handles, they pushed them open. Mom's was inside with two beautiful black women by his side. One was combing his hair and the other was giving him a pedicure. They both wore pink one-piece mini-dresses that read, *"Moms little girl"* in purple letters.

His hair was permed and fell down his back. And his extra light skin and girl like features made him look like the singer Prince. They called him Mom's because if you didn't pay your debt your mother would be the first person he killed. Mom's was deep in the drug game and dealt mainly in prescription drugs although he was trying to wiggle his way into coke. He had access to some of the major drug manufacturing companies and supplied half of DC and Maryland with Vicodin, Oxycontin and other major medicines.

"What brings you here? You know I like Sundays wit' my girls."

"I know and this won't be long," Bricks said walking up to him as Mom's sat in a large chair with two brass lion heads on each side. "I need to find somebody and I know you know everything."

Mom's smiled and said, "Got my money?"

Bricks dug in his pocket, peeled off five hundred dollars and placed it in a plate next to the door, which set on a pedestal.

"Okay, son, what's his name?"

Bricks looked at Yvonna and she said, "S...Swoopes. His name is Swoopes."

"Swoopes?" He repeated and readjusted in the seat. "What's his government name?"

"I don't know. We aren't friends. We never were."

"You gotta give me something more to go off."

"Look, tell him what you know," Bricks said nudging her arm.

"All I know is...he runs with a crew called the YBM."

"Stop!" he said holding his hand out. The women who were pampering him ceased their actions and sat at his feet. "The Young Black Millionaires?"

"Yes."

"Is he missing a left eye?" She nodded yes. "And three fingers from his right hand?"

"Yes."

Moms looked around, stood up and walked over to them. "Why do you want to find him?"

"A long story." Bricks told him. "But it's urgent that I touch him...I mean...get in touch with him."

"I'll tell you where you can find him, but I want you to take care of him too." He said with an evil glare.

"What's in it for you?" Moms grabbed the money Bricks placed in his offering plate and handed it to Yvonna.

"He got into a fight with my nephew Corn who was in FCI with him doing a bid. They ended up shipping my nephew to another prison where he was later shanked and killed. They tried to say my nephew turned states which was why they shipped him, but I know that's some bullshit. So I want Swoopes dead," he said firmly, "had Swoopes never fought my nephew, he'd still be alive."

"I'll take care of him," Bricks said. "So where can I find this dude?"

"It ain't gonna be as easy as you think to get a hold of him. But sit down, I'ma tell you all I know."

COLD CASE

The old-style radiator heater rattled in the cheap motel room and the dark brown curtains stirred, drying up the leftover pizza in the box. It was hot, and the staleness of the room was thick. It served as the meeting place for the unofficial task force of cops, ex's and psychiatrists who had all been burned by Yvonna.

"So what are we going to do? She's home now?" Peter asked sitting at the brown wooden table. "It's just a matter of time before she comes for us."

"I don't think she will," Terrell's said, his 6'4 inch frame paced the floor. His biracial background gave his skin a bronze tone and he looked like a model amongst them. "I think we should stay with the plan. If we move off the plan, things can get out of hand."

"Stay on the plan for what? To find this Gabriella girl who probably died a long time ago?" Lily asked sipping her ice-cold coffee as she sat across from Peter. "How is finding her significant anyway? To me it feels like a waste of time."

He stopped looked down at her and said, "If we must haunt our prey, we should at least know the species. That's why." Terrell was irritated.

"Well have you found anything that will help?" Guy asked. "Cause I'm with Lily, I think we should kill her and get it over with. She's not pregnant now and the hit man won't have a problem finishing what he started. Since that was the only reason he didn't finish her off to begin with."

"I have a meeting with the preacher at the church where Gabriella first showed up. I should be able to find out something then."

"This is so fuckin' stupid!" Lily yelled. "

"Either we do it this way or count me out," Terrell said.

"Oh...oh...I get it," Lily said walking up to him. "You're still in love. You still think you can change her. After all these years you haven't gotten over the fact that she's crazy. What's goin' on, Jona, you ain't fuckin' him hard enough?" She laughed.

Terrell slapped her and she placed her hand on her face. The heat from the blood rushing to her skin warmed her hand.

"I don't' love her anymore." He said not bothering to apologize. "But don't fuck with me on this." He grabbed his things and was preparing to leave without his fiancé. "I'll let you all know when I find out something."

"We're not going to wait for her to come after us," Lily said before he had a chance to leave. "Because she killed my partner and a lot of other people and I haven't forgotten. Even if you have."

He looked at everyone one last time, and stormed out the room.

A FULL MOON

Bricks walked into his house with Yvonna close on his heels after their visit with Mom's. Bricks had already sent a few of his boys to the block Mom's said Swoopes and his men frequented, but he didn't have his home address. Outside of roughing up a few dudes, they still couldn't find Swoopes. When he walked inside, it was quiet and he saw Bet's overnight bag on the floor. Michelle "Bet" Blake, was Kendal's mother and she'd also given birth to Chomps. And the story behind the boy's birth was strange enough for an entire show on Maury Povich.

A year ago, Bet's only son Mitch K. Blake, nicknamed "Deuce" had married his high school sweetheart Karen Dexter. Karen couldn't have children of her own and both her and Deuce wanted a child. So badly that in the beginning, it was the only reason they argued. Bet, feeling bad for her son, agreed to carry their child to full term.

Before Bet had a chance to change her mind, Deuce and Karen went to a fertility clinic where Karen's egg was retrieved from her body and induced with Deuce's sperm. Against the doctor's orders, the forty-two year old woman amazingly got pregnant and carried their baby to full term. But a week after their son Theodore "Chomps" Blake was born; Karen discovered Deuce was seeing someone else whom he planned to leave her for. Karen's entire world was rocked having walked in on them in her bedroom making love.

Karen not able to accept living without him, called him from her mother's house, who was out of town on business. Deuce agreed to meet her there and when he walked through the door, she hugged him, cried in his arms, and put a bullet through her head. She died as he held her, while he soaked in her blood.

It took him minutes to regain his composure long enough to see the blood stained note in her left hand. It read, *'Everything I do is for you. If there is no you, there is no me. I hope your new relationship makes you happy. But if you still want to be with me, like I do with you, I left one more bullet in the gun. Be with me for eternity.'*

Deuce was overwhelmed with guilt and without thinking about Chomps, picked the gun up and put a bullet through his forehead. Their life story was very full and filled with secrecy.

"Hey Bricks, where's Kendal?" Bet asked appearing from the back of the house. Chomps rested on her hips with his bottle in his hands.

"I'm puttin' Kendal out."

Bet shook her head and sat on the couch. "What she do this time?" she asked looking at the baby.

"A long story, a lot of shit went down since you been gone. It ain't safe no more so you may have to stay someplace else too."

"I see," she said looking at Yvonna. "So tell me, who's

this young lady?"

Although she wanted an answer, her tone was kind and warm. She wasn't as rude and nasty as her daughter.

"Somebody I need to help clear some things out. But did you hear what I said? You and Kendal are going to have to find someplace else to stay."

"You know I can take care of me but I'm more concerned about you."

Yvonna saw something in her eyes and although she couldn't be sure, she felt a connection between Bet and Bricks. After all, Bet was bad to be forty-something. The only sign of age was in her eyes.

"It's time to start lookin' Bet. This was only temporary anyway."

"Aight," she said placing Chomps on the floor. "But you know I'm always away and Kendal has nowhere to go. Her credit is too fucked up to get a place of her own, and I don't have a legal job."

"That's ya'll problem not mine, Bet." Bet's eyes saddened and she looked at Yvonna. She was wondering how much she'd know about her and her family. Bricks caught her stare and said, "Don't worry, she doesn't know anything."

Bet exhaled and said, "We're not ready, Bricks. You help out a lot with the baby and he needs to be around another man. Please...don't do this to us."

As he was saying that Chomps crawled over to him and Bricks bent down and picked him up. "He can stay. My cousin Tina watches him all the time anyway, but I want ya'll out by the end of the week. Kendal's been wildin' out and I had to lay hands on her earlier. I can't take it no more."

Bet removed the baby from his arms and placed him down. Pulling Bricks closer she said, "I need you...please."

He pushed away from her and yelled, "You and that bitch don't fuckin' get it! I'm sick wit' all this drama in my crib. You got a week and after that I want you out! Don't make me say it again."

When Yvonna followed him, she made a mistake of looking behind her once, and when she did, Bet gave her an evil glare. It was one she wouldn't forget.

I LIKE 'EM SHORT HAIR-BROWN-THICK-BONED

"Get on the floor!" Swoopes told the prostitute he picked up earlier that day. He sat on an old bed at his cousin Cane's crib, took off the shade from a lamp, and placed it on the floor at his feet. "Right there." He pointed.

The naked young pretty black girl, who he called Newbie, did as she was told, but there was fear in her eyes. After all, this was her first time with a john and she hoped things went smoothly. Most of all, she hoped she'd have enough money to give to her pimp, Xodus, who was a self-proclaimed woman beater. On her hands and knees she nervously awaited his next command.

"Lay back, and open your legs."

Again she obeyed, and the cheap carpet fibers dug into her soft skin. Swoopes looked down at her salaciously. It turned him on to see small red heart tattoos starting at her ankle, growing larger as they moved up to her pussy.

"Open wider." She complied, able to see his partial disgust and lust for her all at the same time.

Newbie ran away from her preacher father a few months earlier, because she hated being under his strict supervision. With her mother dying a long time ago due to alcoholism, she embraced the streets heavily.

"You like that shit don't you? Lying on the floor, with your legs opened in front of niggas you don't know." She agreed. "Put your finger in your pussy. And do it nice and slow."

Newbie, moved her fingers slowly in and out of her pussy, something she did on the regular at home. Bucking her tiny hips, she widened her thick legs showing him her hairless box. She was on the verge of an orgasm and Swoopes stood in amazement as her cave got wetter and wetter.

She bit down on her bottom lip as her lower body shivered in pleasure. She never stopped looking at him as she yielded to his command. Her finger strokes got deeper and deeper as her legs spread wider apart. And after each exit, she massaged her throbbing clit.

"Ummmmmm...mmmmmmm," she moaned, eyes still glued onto Swoopes.

"Damn, girl. That shit sexy," he said standing over top of her, removing himself from his pants. "Keep doin' that shit."

Her body began to quiver all over and her toes spread a little as she mentally escaped into her own world. For that moment, she was alone.

"Ahhhhh..." she moaned. She was a *squirter* and cum flew from her body. She had came, and her shivers became less and less intense. She reached an orgasm in front of him, and he liked her instantly. She was an exhibitionist, naive and young...his favorite combination.

"You came didn't you?" He asked now stroked to a full thickness. He eyed the silky white oil on her hands.

"N...no." she lied, shaking her head. "I was just doin' that for you."

His outrage covered his face like a mask and he said, "So you lyin' to me? If there's one thing I hate, a liar is it. You gonna make me hate you? Is that what you want?"

"No. I mean...yes...Yes I did cum."

"Why you lie? You like bein' a liar and a slut?" He asked hammering her about irrelevancies. He was building up anger and rage because he liked sex better that way. "I hate a fuckin' liar." He didn't see Newbie's face anymore he saw Yvonna.

Without waiting on her response he got on his hands and knees, turned her over and spread her legs apart. Then he entered her tight ass as roughly as possible. She screamed out in pain and he covered her mouth with his hand.

"You a stupid bitch ain't you, Yvonna? Like fuckin' up nigga's lives huh?"

In and out, in and out he moved inside of her until he felt his hammer pulsating inside of her warm body. Nothing was going to stop him but himself. Her legs trembled as he released her mouth, rose up, and pushed deeper inside of her warmth. She tightened up in agony and that felt even better to him. In and out, in and out he pushed into her softness until he exploded.

When he was done, she rolled over and covered her body with her hands.

"Get up and put your clothes on." The moment he said that his cell phone rang and he answered. "Who is it?"

"It's me, Rook."

"What?" Swoopes asked, adjusting his pants. "I'm busy."

"Some niggas been 'round here askin' 'bout you. Bobby and Ruese dead."

Swoopes stopped moving and looked out into the room. "Fuck you talkin' 'bout?"

"'Bout five dudes came through the block and killed Bobby and Ruese. You think it's that bitch?"

"Can, I have my money?" Newbie asked now fully dressed. Her short spiky hair not as neat as it was when he first picked her up. "I gotta get goin'. My daddy's gonna be mad if I don't bring him his money."

He put his finger up indicating for her to wait. "So what ya'll do?"

"We bucked at 'em but it was too many of 'em. And the block we were on, I don't even know how they found out about it. It's Mike's spot in Takoma and you know that joint low-key."

"So ya'll ain't hit nothin' or nobody?" Swoopes asked not caring about anything else.

"No."

It fucked him up that he had threatened Bricks and he still didn't go away. Usually people took his warnings seriously but with Bricks it was another story. He'd have to deal with him gangsta to gangsta. "I'm on my way. Let me know if anybody comes back around."

When he hung up he said, "Newbie, you comin' wit' me."

She was frightened and said, "But...but I can't. If I don't get back, Xodus will kill me."

"Fuck that nigga. You wit' me now. Got it?"

"I just want my money so I can go home. He just took me back and will put me out again."

He walked up to her and gripped her arms. Slowly,

she looked up at his eye patch and violently quivered under his touch. He was terrifying and she wished she never left with him, but wishing wouldn't do her any good at that moment.

"If you knew me, you wouldn't push it. Now, the life you had is over. You go where I go and as far as you know, I'm everything to you, including home. Matta fact, you can call me God."

SPOTTED

"I think that's the house Mom's was talking about. He said it would look outta place on the block. Now that I think about it, I remember Bilal telling me Swoopes spent a lot of time over his cousin Cane's house, because he was never here."

"Aight," Bricks said surveying the old green house under the night sky. "I think that's his car too."

Yvonna looked at it a few cars ahead and said, "Yep. He's in there." The grounds were unkempt and the grass was three feet tall.

"Somebody's comin' out," Yvonna said sinking into her seat when the house door flew open.

"Is that him?" Bricks asked, grabbing his weapon. He loaded it and ducked a little in his seat.

"I...I think so." Her heart raced and she silently hoped everything would be over soon. Swoopes walked to his car, looked around quickly and got inside.

"He got some bitch wit' him," Bricks said to no one in particular. "She in the wrong place at the wrong time."

Newbie opened the passenger door and got into the car. The moment she shut the door, Bricks hurriedly got out to catch him before he pulled off. Running toward Swoopes' back window, he fired once into the glass, aiming for his head. The bullet caused minimal damage as it ricocheted off of the car, crashing into a streetlight behind him.

"What the fuck!?" Swoopes said looking around after hearing the impact.

Although the street was now darker, when Bricks rose, Swoopes saw him in his rearview mirror. He smiled, and presented him with the "Fuck You" sign before he pulled off. He had gotten away.

"Fuck! Fuck! Fuck!" He screamed, firing two more bullets at the car.

But it was too late; Swoopes was gone with the wind. Frustrated, he placed his gun under his shirt and jogged back to the car.

"What happened?" Yvonna asked when he got inside. "Why he get away?"

"The car was bulletproof. What kinda shit this nigga into, where he gots to have a bulletproof car?" Yvonna sat quietly in her seat shaking her head. "What's wrong wit' you?" He asked pulling off slowly heading back to his house. "I'ma get this nigga."

"Did he see you?" She was fucked up with him for starting something and not finishing it.

"Yeah," he said hesitantly.

"*Well*...I hope you know that all hell is getting ready to break loose now."

"Where you been?" he smirked looking at her. "Hell broke loose when the nigga came to my crib. It's just time for war."

THE INEVITABLE

Penny had just put Delilah down to bed when the house phone rang.

"Hello." She whispered walking toward the living room. She flipped on the light switch and sat on her recliner.

"Penny Hightower?" A woman's voice called.

"Who is this?"

"It's Jona, Yvonna's psychiatrist."

"Oh...uh...what can I do for ya?"

"Is Yvonna there? We have an appointment tomorrow and I want to make sure she'll be here. I called earlier, but no one answered the phone and I didn't hear a voicemail."

"Well I ain't got one."

"I understand. I'm just calling to confirm our meeting. I really am sorry to bother you."

"Look, I'm not tryin' to get all tied up into this so I'ma be straight wit' ya. Yvonna ain't been here for two days. Ya'll may have to come get her because I can't control her."

"But as a condition of her release, you agreed to let her stay there."

"Yvonna's a grown woman and I ain't her keeper. I been keepin' this here baby by myself since she been in the institution and she 'bout the only-est one I can be responsiba for. Now I have a man now, and I have to 'tend to him upstairs. Okay?"

"Ms. Hightower, I'm happy you have a man, and by your mention of him I take it it's been a long time. But please let Yvonna know that if she isn't here tomorrow, I will alert the authorities."

"Well I'm sure she won't like you threatnin' her."

"At this point, I could care less what she likes. Have a nice day."

Penny ended the call and could tell there was animosity in Jona's voice. She was certain that Yvonna had rubbed her the wrong way like she did everybody. She was also certain that if the woman didn't ease up, she'd be introduced to trouble that she wouldn't be able to get away from.

DARK NIGHT

Yvonna's heart pounded in her chest, as they got closer to Brick's house. She knew Swoopes well enough to know that Brick's *miss*, was probably fatal for both of them.

Even though it was late, she decided to call Penny's house and she prayed Delilah was still up as it may be the last time she ever got to speak to her.

"Who's this?" Penny asked.

"It's me, Yvonna. I'm sorry to wake you, Penny."

She sighed and said, "I'm already up. That Jona lady just called my house. Who calls somebody house so late at night anyways? Plain stupid!"

"I'm sorry about that. What did she say?"

"She said you have an appointment tomorrow and you gots to go, or they gone pick you up." She sighed. "I hope you plan on 'tendin' 'cause she sounded irritated by the whole situation."

"She know I'm not there? At the house with you?"

"Oh...uh...Naw. I ain't tell her nothin'." Penny lied.

"That's yo business not mine. Why would you even ask me somethin' like that anyway, chile?"

"I'm sorry. I just got a lot of stuff goin' on. Is Delilah up?"

"No. I put her down a hour ago."

"Can you tell her I love her, the moment she get's up?"

"I guess so, course I usually feeds her first."

"For me," Yvonna said feeling like her relationship with her daughter was in jeopardy. "Please."

"Well, alright, chile. 'Spose I can. When you comin' home?"

"Soon."

"Alright...I'll see you when I do." She abruptly hung up the phone.

"Bye." Yvonna said looking at the cell phone strangely.

She thought it was weird that Penny got off the phone so quickly because normally she'd be the one who'd have to hang up first. But for some reason, Penny had rushed her off the line like she was irritating her.

"Everything cool?" Bricks asked interrupting her thoughts.

"No." She looked out her window at the houses they passed. "Just stuff I gotta deal with at home."

"Look, you'll be able to go home soon. I know you wanna see your kid."

"I can't go until this is over." She sighed. "I guess I'm safer with you."

"I feel you," he said looking over at her. "Outside of all this shit, what's up wit' you? You seem out of it."

"Bricks, this is enough shit to fuck anybody's mind up. What I really want to know is...are you gonna protect me?"

"On my life...ain't shit gonna happen to you, as long as you stay wit' me."

She exhaled as they turned onto the street leading to his house. And when they did, she saw a car parked in the middle of the street. Her heart raced and she wondered if it was one of Swoopes men.

"Oh my, God! He found us! He's gonna kill us."

"Calm down," he said reaching for the car door. "I'll be right back. Just chill out for a sec'."

"Where you goin'?"

"Yo, Yvonna, be easy, ma," he said seriously. "I said I'll be back."

Bricks exited the car and walked toward the parked vehicle. When he was a few feet away, the man got out and embraced Bricks in a one armed hug. They exchanged a few words and Yvonna sighed in relief. A few minutes later, Bricks returned to the car.

The driver in the middle of the street moved to let them through, and when they passed, the man parked back in the middle of the street. They had the block on lock. As they drove down the street, there were men standing in front of the houses like soldiers. They waved at Bricks as he passed before he parked in front of his house.

"You know all of them people?"

"I know every nigga on this block. I told you...you safe with me."

"What do you do? For real?"

"Let's just say I'm worth a lot of money." He smiled.

After she dated Bilal, she dealt with milder men and forgot how good it felt to be in the presence of a boss. The more time she spent with Bricks, the more she was starting to realize that there were more things she liked about him than she knew.

When they walked into the house, they saw Kendal in the kitchen, cutting apples. "Can I talk to you for a minute?" Kendal asked Bricks.

"Why are you even here? You should be gettin' your shit together. I'm not fuckin' around; I want you gone by the end of the week."

"Please listen, Bricks. I found out somethin' about your little girlfriend," she said as she walked up to him. "She's fuckin' crazy, Bricks! She's taken some Clozaril shit and I found out from the pharmacist today that it's for schizophrenia. I bet she ain't tell you that did she?" Bricks looked at Yvonna and back at Kendal.

"You just can't fuckin' stop!" He said not believing her. "It don't matter, you not stayin' here tonight." He walked to the kitchen. "Now I'm tryin' to be easy, but you gonna make me leap on you."

"Bricks, what I'm saying is true! I care 'bout you, even if you don't want me."

Bricks ignored her as he opened the refrigerator, grabbed a beer and gulped it down. Visions of wrapping his hands around Kendal's throat danced through his head.

Yvonna feeling outta place walked into the kitchen behind him and quietly asked, "Can I go downstairs? I wanna lie down."

He removed the beer from his lips and with his eyes firmly on Kendal said, "Yeah. I'll be down in a sec."

"Bitch, you ain't doin' shit!" Kendal yelled blocking her path. "Tell him what I'm sayin' is true. Tell him you fuckin' crazy!"

"Look, I don't want no trouble." She said walking to the left of her. Kendal blocked her again. "I just wanna go downstairs."

"Bitch, I ain't tryin' to hear all that. Go 'head, let him

see what you really are. Let him see what I'm sayin' is true."

"Please, I just want to..."

Before she could finish her sentence she smacked Yvonna in the face so hard, she temporarily forgot where she was. But she remembered quickly.

"Now what, bitch?" Kendal chided.

"If you don't get the FUCK outta my face, I'ma gut your ass," Gabriella said in a low deep voice.

When Kendal looked down, she saw the knife she used to cut the apple, held closely against her stomach.

"Hold up...I...I."

"Bitch, you not hearin' me," Gabriella continued poking her, cutting her skin slightly. "I said get your black ass out my fuckin' face!"

When Kendal ran to the sofa, and looked at Bricks in horror, Yvonna dropped the knife. When she looked back at Bricks, she noticed he was motionless. Yvonna had come back to reality only to realize that what she was so desperately trying to get away from, had caught up to her.

"Look, I'm sorry, Bricks. But I gotta go," she said as she ran out the door, and into the night.

DISGRACEFUL
LEADERSHIP

Swoopes pushed past the extra high grass and empty beer bottles to get to the door of his run down house in Northwest DC. Newbie was right behind him. When he opened the door, he was irritated to see children's toys in his path. Toys flew from left to right as he kicked them out his lane.

"Where the fuck is Crystal?" He asked referring to his girlfriend who he'd gotten into an argument with earlier.

"She just said she was goin' to the store," Cane said looking at Newbie as if something were wrong. He knew if Crystal came in and Newbie was standing there, it would take all six men to pull her up off her. "But she took some clothes with her so she might be out all night. Is everything 'aight, man?"

Six of his men were there including his cousin Cane and Growl, the man who would kill on command for him. Growl was dangerous and uncontrollable and Swoopes liked him that way.

Cane on the other hand was calmer and was in charge of their growing drug operation. He was the level-headed one out of the crew.

"Oh yeah, everything cool, 'cept for the fact that the nigga tried to creep me today."

"At my place?" Cane questioned.

"Yeah. I don't know how the fuck they knew where you lived."

"Remember she's Bilal's ex-girl," Cane offered. "You know he told her everything."

Swoopes sat in a tattered black recliner by the door. "How long Crystal been gone?"

"'Bout fifteen minutes," Cane said walking up to the door.

"Cool, is the internet workin' yet? I gotta set Newbie here up on what I need her to do."

"Yeah...it's all set up and ready." Cane said.

"Cool."

The house smelled old and stale and because most of the YBM used it as a clubhouse instead of Swoopes' home, there was no sign of decorative taste anywhere in sight. The cream couch was dingy and pushed against the dirty white wall, and the screen TV sat on the floor connected to a Playstation 3. The only other furniture in the room was a glass table that was so grimey, you couldn't see through it. On top of it sat ashtrays, beer cans and blunts.

"On some otha shit, the connect called, son. He said you didn't get that," Growl said not sure if she should speak in front of Newbie. He felt he had to say something though, because missing the connect meant not meeting demand. "He said he tried to call you but couldn't get an answer. You want me to call him back?"

"Naw. He good. I just ain't go," he said under his breath. He couldn't tell his men that he'd forgotten the meeting due to being so obsessed with finding Yvonna, "I'll get up with him later."

Newbie pushed a few game controllers over on the couch and softly said, "God, can I go to the bathroom?" Everyone looked at her in disbelief because of what she called him. "Yeah...hurry up, it's down the hall. You got five minutes." He smiled.

When she left Growl walked up to him and said, "What's up wit' that? Shawty fire but you know Crystal gonna flip if she catch her up in here."

"Fuck Crystal!" He spat. "She should take care of home and she wouldn't have to worry."

"I feel you," he backed off. "But what you gonna do 'bout the connect? He said if you don't come today, fuck it."

Swoopes looked at him and frowned, "Well if his white ass don't wanna make no money, fuck him! We'll get another connect."

Cane looked at Growl and tried to diffuse the situation. He knew once Swoopes heard what the connect said, he'd be mad and may jump to an erratic conclusion, "He didn't say that," Cane said looking at Growl not wanting him to say another word, "he said he wanted to make sure you kept the next appointment. You know how busy he is, Swoopes. But you know he appreciate the paper too."

"Well I'm busy, too!" Swoopes yelled.

"Yeah, wit' runnin' behind that bitch," Chavis said, to another YBM member. He had been drinking so much that he didn't realize how loud he was, but he would soon find out.

Cane and Growl looked at Chavis, and Swoopes walked over to him. Chavis backed up into a wall that wouldn't allow him go any further. He was young and unlike the older members, he didn't have much respect for Swoopes. Chavis felt he was more consumed with Yvonna than business. Back in the day, when Swoopes was locked up, it was fashionable to talk about him, but things had changed.

When Swoopes was within the breathing space of Chavis he gave him a murderous stare. He wanted him to see that no matter what he had heard in the past, the part about him being a cold-blooded killer was all true.

"You got somethin' you wanna get off your chest, young?"

Chavis shook his head no and said, "Naw...I'm cool."

"Well it sounded like you had so much to say a minute ago, so how 'bout you say that shit to my face."

"I'm...I'm sorry, man. It wasn't really like that. I was drinkin' and fucked up."

Swoopes could see his marshmallow center, and knew that it wouldn't take the D.A. no time to break him if he got caught up.

"So you always fuck up when you drinkin'?" He took the beer out of his hand and poured it on his head slowly. "Maybe you shouldn't fuck wit' it then."

The liquid ran down his face and onto his jacket. The men knew that Chavis' future in the YBM was over.

"And what the fuck is this?" He asked pulling at the black North Face jacket with the letters YBM stitched on the sleeve. "Ya'll still rockin' these?" He looked at his men.

"Naw, cuz, just the new ones," Cane said feeling pity for the young member.

"Well startin' today I don't wanna see nobody wit'

one of these on!" He said looking behind him. "This ain't doin' nothin' but beggin' the cops to fuck wit' us." Then he looked back at Chavis. "Take that shit off." Chavis moved so quickly, his arm got jammed in one of the sleeves and he fought with himself to get it off. Swoopes laughed at his antics. "Can you cook young blood? And clean?"

"Y...yes."

"Now that's good, cause my girl can't cook or clean worth shit. So from here on out, you my personal bitch. When I wake up, my breakfast better be ready, when I go out in the afternoon, my lunch better be on the table and at night, my dinner betta neva be late. You got that?"

"Yes."

"Yes what?" He said turning his head so that Chavis could say it in his ear.

"Yes, sir."

"Good, and then I want you to make sure the house is clean. Pick up all this shit," he said pushing stuff around. "I'm sick of the place lookin' like this."

The humiliation Chavis felt showed all over his face and his crew members could no longer in good conscious, look at the pathetic scene.

"Now get in there and make me a pack of them noodles. Put some eggs in 'em too." Chavis looked at Swoopes and then at Cane and Growl. "Fuck is you lookin' at them for? Move!"

When Chavis tended to his womanly duties, Swoopes looked at his men.

"Anybody else got somethin' they wanna get off they chest?" No one breathed a word. "I ain't think so."

Just when he said that Newbie came out and said, "God, can I wash up? I just got my girl day."

Swoopes smiled and said, "Yeah...and when you finish, I'ma put these niggas out so I can let you suck my
dick."

BACK TO THE BASICS

The night temperature had dropped and it was cooler than it was a few hours earlier. But Yvonna's blood was boiling so hot, she couldn't tell. She ran as far as she could away from Brick's house. Warm tears dried against her face as the wind smacked her skin. She was an emotional wreck.

Brick's men watched as the anxious girl ran away. Her cell phone rang and she didn't bother answering because she knew it was him and the embarrassment she felt wouldn't allow her to.

"I would tell you to stop running, but after looking at your fat ass, I'd say you should run another fifteen minutes." Gabriella laughed. "Damn, Yvonna, how could you let things get so bad?"

Yvonna heard her voice behind her, but chose to ignore it.

"Come on now, you gotta talk to somebody," she said slyly. "Might as well be yourself."

"Go away!" Yvonna yelled, scaring a dog bouncing

around in his yard.

"Yvonna, everyone has alter egos. Even the so called sane. Be glad your's just saved you because the way that bitch back there was going on you, I thought I was watching a scene from that show 'Oz'."

"Shut up!"

"You were five seconds from washing that girl's dirty draws."

Yvonna continued to ignore her and when she reached the end of Brick's block, she made a left and than a right onto the next street.

"Do you have any idea of how weak you are right now?"

"You're not here. You're not real."

"You're right, Yvonna. I'm not real to *them*, but I'm very real to you." She paused. "I'm your strength. Why would you let them take that away from you?"

Yvonna's breath was getting thicker and she was finding it difficult to run any further. So she stopped and bent over to catch her breath. And as she looked to her left she saw a brick house, and behind it, sat another house with a little girl playing on her back porch. The back door was open and something came over her.

"Go 'head. It's just a matter of time before Bricks comes looking for you. Don't be stupid. Go." In survivor mode, she passed the first house, jumped over the fence and walked up to the little girl in the backyard.

"What you playin' wit'?" Yvonna asked with a sinister smile, breathing heavily. "You look like you having fun."

"My doll." The little girl replied showing her. "It's my favorite."

"That's nice. I had a doll just like that when I was your age. The exact same one. Can I see?"

"But...my grandmother made this for me." The child was greatly suspicious. As well as she should've been, Yvonna was a fucking lunatic. "It's the only one like it."

"Way to go, idiot!" Gabriella yelled walking beside the little girl. "Instead of just yokin' her young ass up, you wanna play Mister Rogers Neighborhood. Now you done said the wrong shit and this little bitch called you on it."

Yvonna closed her eyes and shook her head to get Gabriella's voice out of her mind. But she could still see her wearing a pair jeans and a black leather coat standing right next to her.

"I'm not paying you any attention," she said out loud. "Is your mother home?" she asked the child. "I'm her friend and I have something to give her."

"She's in her room. She hardly ever comes out."

"Awww...I bet you want somebody to play with don't you?" She nodded in agreement. "You know what, I have a little girl too who would love to play with you. Would you like that?"

Gabriella made a loud snoring sound in her ear. "Bitch, speed this shit up, please! You 'bout to put both our asses to sleep."

"Shut up!" Yvonna said looking at her.

The moment she did, she regretted it. But the longer she went without her medicine, the more she was susceptible to hallucinations.

"Who are you talking to?" The girl asked.

"My imaginary friend. I bet you have one too don't you."

"No!" the little girl shook her head. "That's crazy."

Yvonna stood up straight and frowned. "Is anyone else inside?"

"No...just mama."

"Okay, let's go and surprise her."

They walked into the house and Yvonna stopped at the kitchen to grab a butcher knife. After examining its sharpness, she took it. "What's that for?"

"I'm gonna play a trick on your mother. I'm gonna make her think I'm going to hurt her if she doesn't give me what I want, but for real I won't. It'll just be our little secret. Are you good with secrets?" The little girl nodded. "Good. Me too. Let's go." When they walked to her mother's room, Yvonna said, "Knock on the door and call her name."

The girl knocked twice and a woman's voice yelled, "What the fuck do you want? I told you to leave me the fuck alone! I need to get some sleep before I go out!"

"That bitch is wretched," Gabriella laughed. "I love her!"

"Knock again." Yvonna said. "I need her to open the door. It's the only way I can surprise her good."

The girl shook her head and said, "No....no! She's gonna beat me."

For some reason, Yvonna felt the little girl's plight. She knew how it felt to be alone and scared. After all, she dealt with extreme loneliness and abandonment as a child all her life.

"Listen," Yvonna said stooping down. "If that bitch touches, you, I'll break every last bone in her body. Okay? Now knock on the door." The girl's eyes widened with shock and Yvonna said, "Go 'head. This'll be good."

She nodded quickly and knocked on the door again.

"You know what...," the woman started. Yvonna could hear the bed squeak and her feet slap against the floor. She was quickly approaching the door until she flung it open and said, "I'm gonna kill your black ass!"

The moment her big toe crossed the threshold,

Yvonna whacked her in the face with a closed fist. The woman fell flat on her back and tried to get up but she was too fucking slow. Yvonna rushed over her and put the knife against her neck.

"Listen, your daughter and me are just playin' a game. If you play along wit' us, everything will go smooth," Yvonna said smiling at the little girl behind her. She was trying to calm her down so that she wouldn't run out the front door and tell someone her murderous ass was in there. When she was sure she won the girl over, Yvonna looked sinisterly at the woman beneath her. "So play along and no one will get hurt."

"You broke my nose!" the woman screamed holding her bleeding sniffer. Yvonna stood up, took her foot and slammed it down on her nose again. "Ahhhhhhhhhhh! What the fuccccccccccccck?!" She screamed in pain, as she lie flat on her back. "I...I can't breathe!"

"Good, bitch! If you say somethin' else, I'ma consider you a lost cause. Now you fuckin' playin' with us or not?"

"Y...yes."

"Good. Where is your money?"

"I...got...a...couple bucks in my purse," she pointed toward the nightstand next to the bed. A fake Gucci with the thread coming out of it sat open on top of it. "That's all I got."

"She got some money under her bed too," the little girl offered.

The woman rose up in a sitting position and said, "I'ma beat your ass. Wait 'till this all is over." The girl was so frightened, her stomach rumbled and she released gas. Yvonna wasn't in the hero business but she couldn't help but feel for her new friend. Not to mention she held back on the cash. Yvonna decided that she had to pay...with her life.

"You got a daddy?" She asked the little girl. "Or somebody to take care of you?"

"Wait...what you 'bout to do?"

Yvonna kicked the woman in the teeth and a tooth flew out of her mouth.   "Say one more thing and you won't be alive long enough to feel pain again."

"What's up, kid? Do you got a daddy or not?"

"Yes."

"You love him?" Yvonna asked staring down at the woman and then back at her. "I'ma need you to think long and hard before you answer me on this one."

The little girl paused and said, "Uh...he's real nice. And my cousin too."

"That's all I needed to know," Yvonna said before dropping to her knees and slicing the woman's throat. The woman grabbed at her neck before allowing her arms to fall by her sides. "'Cause you gonna live wit' him now."

At first the girl was frightened, and backed against a small table, causing a picture to fall to the floor. But her mother had abused her so much, that the child appeared happy that she wouldn't have to worry about her anymore.

"Now, don't be sad, I just did you a favor." Yvonna wiped the blood from the blade on the back of her pants. "You might not understand it now but you will later."

"You back! That's what the fuck I'm talkin' 'bout," Gabriella cheered. "Now we can finally finish what we started."

Yvonna grabbed the money in the woman's purse and under the bed and the little girl followed behind her. When she walked into the small pink bathroom, she found a perm, which she used and some dye for her hair. She put them both in and cut her hair back short in her trademark style. With it still wet, she located some hair gel and laid the smooth black strands down neatly. Lastly Yvonna wiped the house down thoroughly and vacuumed up the hair in all the places she'd been. When she was done, she removed the vacuum bag. She was taking it with her to prevent forensics from finding evidence. The little girl stayed two feet next to her the entire time.

"How you doin', kid? You gonna be okay when I leave?" Yvonna asked.

"Yes. I think so."

"You got your daddy's number?" She nodded. "Good call him when I leave. Now...we need to go over our plan. If someone asks you, you never saw a woman. If they ask you how the person looked who played a game with you, tell them it was a man. Can I trust you?"

"Yvonna if you don't kill this kid I will," Gabriella yelled appearing to her left. "I'm not 'bout to let you leave a witness. Kill the little bastard and let's go."

"Shut the fuck up, Gabriella. You ain't doin' shit!" Yvonna screamed.

When she turned back to the child she said, "Is that your imaginary friend again?"

"Yeah." Yvonna said embarrassed she let Gabriella get her so angry, that she couldn't compose herself.

"Why is she so mean?"

"Fuck you, muppet!" Gabriella howled.

"Cause that's what the bitch does. Listen...we have to get our stories together. I need to know you got this because if you don't, my friend over here is going to make me kill you, and I don't wanna do that."

The little girl looked frightened and said, "Oh...okay, uh...a man hurt my mother."

"That's it," Yvonna smiled believing she was coming along. "Now he was wearing fatigues and a black shirt and had dark skin."

"What's fatigues? I never heard of that before." She asked with a quizzical stare.

"Damn this kid's a fuckin' idiot," Gabriella interjected.

"Fatigues are an army suit. He was wearin' an army suit okay? Can you remember that?" She nodded. "Now what was he wearin'?" Yvonna said slowly. "Remember what I just said, this is important."

"He was wearing...fat...fat...fat uh..." She couldn't pronounce the words correctly.

"You better kill this chick," Gabriella persisted. "If the right child's psychiatrist gets a hold of her, it's a wrap."

Yvonna hated to admit it but she was right. Out of all the kids in the entire world, she had to run into the dumbest. She was already in the house longer than she wanted to be and she couldn't be sure who would stop by. Picking up the knife, she grabbed the little girl's wrist and decided to kill her by slicing them.

"I'm sorry," Yvonna said stooping over her, "but you gonna have to go be wit' your mommy. I can't afford to let you live."

"No...no," the girl said shaking her head. "I don't like her. I don't wanna be with her."

"I know but this is for the best. *My* best."

"Army fa-tees. He was wearing army fa-tees. He had braids like my mommy's boyfriend and dark black skin. He hurt me sometimes and my mommy let him because he gives her money. And instead of being in her room at night, he comes to mine."

Yvonna stood up straight and looked down at the girl. Her version of the events couldn't be fucked with.

"Damn...her young ass came around quick,"

Gabriella said.

"Oh...uh...I guess you got it then," Yvonna said looking at her. She couldn't believe she came off the top
with a story like that. Of course one look in the child's
eyes and she could tell that the story was true. "I'm
'bout to go. Call your father in about fifteen minutes.
Got it?"

She nodded and Yvonna ran out. She still couldn't
believe she was five seconds from killing a kid but she
would have, no questions asked. With the money she
had in her pocket, she jogged away from the neighborhood, and when she was far enough, hailed a cab. She
had one place in mind to escape to, and that was
Ming's.

DIRTY PILLOWS

When Yvonna lifted her head, a huge window with the sun shining against her face caused her head to ache. She rubbed her throbbing temples and looked around the upscale room.

"Whatever hotel room this is, it must be expensive," she said noticing the pricey brown and gold wallpaper and the designer furniture everywhere.

The more she looked around, the more her head hurt so she allowed it to drop on the super king size bed. She was completely naked outside of the Christian Louboutin pumps on her feet, which she didn't remember buying.

Moving around a little, she felt something extremely uncomfortable between her legs. "What the fuck is that?" She asked, as she reached down and removed an empty Heineken beer bottle from her pussy. "Now this shit is getting weirder and weirder by the minute."

Tossing it on the floor, she tried to remember the events of the night before but she couldn't. And then she remembered her doctor's voice from the institution.

'But always...always...take your medicine. If you don't your mind will convince you of the most absurd things and you'll find yourself in the craziest of situations.'

When she looked to her left, she saw Ming lying with her back faced her naked. "I shoulda known your freak ass was involved."

Looking to her right she saw Ming's boyfriend and sprung up in a sitting position. She knew she wasn't in a hotel room when she saw Ming's handsome baby *Boy* in a picture. They were definitely at Ming's house.

"Ming," Yvonna said nudging her. She didn't move. "Ming...get the fuck up!" Yvonna yelled pushing her harder. She was five seconds from punching her in the back when her boyfriend woke up.

"Do ya want me ta call ya Gabriella or Yvonna?" He asked in a thick Jamaican accent.

"What...what are you talking about?" Yvonna asked between quick breaths, her heart palpitating. Full nights of allowing Gabriella to run rampant in her body scared her to death.

"Last night ya asked me and the lady Ming ta call ya Gabriella. And I'm just checking ta see which one it is now."

"My name is Yvonna so call me that." She pulled the covers over her body and an empty Hennessey Black bottle fell to the floor. "And what the fuck happened last night? I don't usually mix Heineken and Hennessey. It's not my speed."

"Well it was ya speed last night. By the way, the name's Darcus." He rose, rubbed his head and walked over to the dresser. His body was so perfect, if a picture was taken of it, you would swear it was photoshopped. Suddenly a brief flash of her sucking his dick while Ming ate her pussy revisited her mind.

"Ya remembered didn't ya?" He asked before he removed a pair of underwear from the drawer. She was still confused by the monstorous size of his dick. "That thang was nice and tight. Just like I like it."

Yvonna tried to be tough and said, "Did you get blood on your dick? Cause I'm supposed to be on my period." The look on his face turned to disgust and she thought it was funny. He went from sexy to being horrified in one instance. "What...you afraid of blood?"

"Blood I'm not afraid of," he said with darkness in his eyes, "but menstrual blood is God's cruel joke. So don't talk to me about such tings."

"So how long have you and Ming been an item?"

"Me and the Lady Ming have an understanding. It's an arrangement that works for both of us. But, I'd like ta talk ta ya privately in the next few days."

"Why?"

"We have business. Don't worry, I'll explain then."

Ming stirred a little, and jumped up. "Ming was out!" She said before she wrapped her hair in a bun with no Bobbie pin. " Why didn't you guys wake Ming up? We could have a little fun before we leave."

"Looks like you had enough fun last night." Yvonna said.

"Ming did. Gabriella was a bad, bad girl, and Ming likes her a lot." Ming got out of bed and swaggered toward Darcus. Even in the daylight Ming's body was flawlessly sexy. "What do you say? One more round?"

"I don't know what happened last night but I have a lot of shit to do today. Penny is tripping and I have to get my car and earn some money to get my baby out of her house," she said looking in Ming's night table drawer for some pain pills. What she saw instead was a copy of Ming's bank statement. "Do...you...have some Tylenol or something, Ming?" She paused catching the digits on the red and white Bank of

America statement. Twenty million dollars? But how?

"It's not in there," Ming said walking toward the bathroom. "Let me go get it for you." Yvonna used this time to look at the statement clearly.

"I don't think ya friend would like ya being nosey."

"What, you gonna tell her?" Yvonna asked looking at him again.

"No, but ya never responded. When can we talk...alone?"

"Never," Yvonna said examining the statement.

"I'm afraid that's not an option," he said in a tone that scared her. "If ya don't make it happen, I will arrange it."

She figured Gabriella must've really put it down on him and now he was tripping. But her attention was refocused on the bank statement. No wonder she could buy Yvonna and her daughter anything she wanted, she was loaded.

Somehow the idea of fucking her from time to time didn't look so bad. What's a little pussy bumping amongst friends? The only problem was, Ming was latchy and she was sure if she fucked Ming like she knew she could, she might have to kill her ass just to get some time alone. She would have to think long and hard before making that move.

What really fucked her up was that she was aware of the one business she owned. And although it was a popular nail salon, she knew it was impossible for her to have that much cash because of it.

"Here you go." Yvonna dropped the statement, slammed the drawer shut and accepted the pill and water. "I couldn't find Tylenol so I brought Advil."

Yvonna took the pill and noticed they were still naked, eyeing her. She could've tested the waters to see if having a Heineken jammed up her ass was the product of a great night of sex, but time wasn't on her side. "Can ya'll please put some clothes on now? I done seen enough cracks this morning to make me broke for five years."

"You scared?" Ming said as she leaned up against Darcus as he massaged her breasts. "You afraid Ming gonna show you another nice time?"

"I'm not even concerned about that. I..."

Yvonna was interrupted when the alarm chimed indicating someone was coming inside Ming's house. Ming screamed, "We have to go! Now!"

"What? Why? What's wrong?" Yvonna asked hopping up, throwing what she believed to be her clothes on.

"Don't ask fucking questions, Yvonna. Just go! There's balcony right over there that leads to lawn. Take it and Ming will be right down. I have to grab car keys."

Yvonna took notice at how quick and smooth Darcus was. Although he was in a hurry, he seemed cool under pressure. Something was definitely up with him. "Ming! Where are you?" A Chinese man's voice yelled from downstairs. He was coming up the stairway quickly. "We must talk now!"

Yvonna, Darcus and Ming ran out onto the balcony, down the stairs and towards Ming's Porsche. Yvonna caught notice of the Chinese driver with a missing ear standing next to a black Lincoln Navigator Limousine. The three of them jumped in Ming's Porsche and she sped off.

"Ming what's going on?" Yvonna asked looking out the back window. An older Chinese man bolted out of Ming's house and ran into the middle of the street to look at the fleeing Porsche. Disgusted that Ming got away, he threw his hands up in the air and walked back to his limousine. "What the fuck you gotten into, Ming?"

"They're my family, it's long story." Her phone rang and she reluctantly answered, "Yes, uncle." Ming said a few words in her native language and hung up the phone.

A tear ran down her face and she aggressively wiped it away. Yvonna thought Darcus was going to comfort her from the back seat, but he was too busy sizing Yvonna up instead, like he always did.

"Well, ladies, I had a great time and I hope ta do this again, soon," he said focusing on Yvonna. "Real soon. For now ya may drop me off at me hotel."

"You okay, Ming?" Yvonna asked placing a hand on her leg. She wanted to help, but didn't want her assistance to be an invitation for more bullshit entering into her life. She had her hands full enough as it was.

"I'm fine." Fifteen minutes later, they pulled up at Extended Stay America, a long-term hotel in Maryland.

"I trust I will see you again," he said looking directly at Yvonna.

"Okay, call me later," Ming said getting out to kiss and hug him.

After they dropped him off Yvonna got right down to it. "Ming, are you gonna at least tell me what the fuck is up? Why we left your house like that? You got more shit with you than I do."

"Ming doubts that very seriously." She said smiling for the first time since having to leave her house in a hurry. "Like Ming said earlier, it was my family. Ming just wasn't in mood to see them. There's much to deal with and not a lot of time."

"You gave your family members a key to your house?"

"Yeah, in case Ming gets locked out."

"Ming, you lyin'. But whatever," Yvonna said realizing she wasn't giving up any information. "So, do you *really* like Darcus?"

"Kinda why?"

"Because for starters he said he wanted to see me

again, and it sounded like it was without you." Ming was silent and Yvonna could tell she struck a nerve.

"We good friends," she sighed, "but Ming wants more. Ming doesn't understand why he seems so distant. Ming does everything for him, but it doesn't work. His attention is elsewhere."

"I'm sorry," Yvonna offered.

"Sorry is for cowards." She said looking at her. "Where am I taking you?"

"I gotta go to my appointment today." She pulled down the visor and looked at her face. "But right now I gotta get some makeup. So take me to CVS real quick."

"CVS? Ming thought you only used Mac."

"Well I can't get to Mac right now, so the cheap shit you use gonna have to do."

When they arrived at CVS, Yvonna went inside, grabbed some gum, some cheap makeup and some perfume. While waiting in the line, she grabbed a magazine and thumbed through it. When she didn't see anything that interested her, she sized a few people up. What was really on her mind was Jona. She wanted to know if she was going to try to pick her brains like she usually did and if she'd be forced to swell on her or not. Deciding that Jona *would* get on her nerves, she made mental notes to tell Ming to stop by the liquor store before taking her to the appointment.

"Hello, Yvonna," a familiar voice said in her ear. He wrapped one arm around her neck like he was whispering sweet nothings to her. "Why don't you put that shit down and come with me?"

"I ain't goin' no fuckin' where with..."

"I think you should re-think that, sexy. We wouldn't wanna problem right here now would we?" he said, his breath smelling of stale cheese.

When she looked down, she saw the tip of a blade between her legs. "Now...do you want me to make them pretty lips between your legs a little deeper, or are you happy with the ones that you got?" She couldn't believe who was doing this to her. Out of all of the people who were hunting her down, this was one person she never saw coming.

"Where we goin'?"

"I'll tell you when we get there."

THE GOOD REVEREND

Terrell walked through the small church and toward the basement to sit at one of the tables. The reverend grabbed a gallon of milk out of the refrigerator, and poured them both a glass. He didn't bother asking Terrell what he wanted to drink, but he was still grateful for the hospitality. The reverend placed the gallon on the table and took a seat.

Playing with the rim of the glass he said, "I appreciate you meeting with me, Pastor Robinson. I know you're busy." He placed his leather briefcase on the table.

"I must tell you I wasn't sure you'd come. You cancelled so many of our appointments I was beginning to think you weren't real." The reverends hair was completely silver and he had deep wrinkles in his face.

"Well, we're talking about Gabriella, who's been missing since forever. It was hard trying to find a good way to talk to you about it. It's been almost thirty years."

The reverend looked away from him, drank all of the milk in his glass, before pouring another. A white milk mustache sat upon his upper lip and he wiped it off.

"You know she told me her last name was Holmes." He laughed.

"Oh really," Terrell scanned the paperwork he gathered and some old newspaper articles he'd pulled from the archive files at the library, "cause I don't remember you telling the police about that last name."

"You don't remember 'cause I didn't tell them. Them police officers had no intentions of finding the little black girl. It wasn't until the ransom we raised that people started taking it seriously."

"Why not? It could've possibly helped in the investigation."

"No it couldn't. Holmes was my son's last name anyway. He took his mother's last name. Gabriella started calling herself that because she liked him that much. We all thought it was puppy love but now I can't be sure. It was rather obsessive."

"You have a son? Where is he?" Terrell asked looking around. "I'd like to meet him especially if he has more information on Gabriella."

"Uh...I don't think that's a good idea."

"Why not? This will help me out a lot."

The pastor sighed and said, "He lives in Simple City, a project in D.C., but I must warn you, he's not going to tell you anything without some money and I'm not talking about a couple of bucks. Lately if he's not getting paid, he doesn't show up for anything and that includes family functions.

"Anyway, when the police came, they questioned him about Gabriella everyday for two weeks. He was the last person who saw her but he never gave up any information. I started to believe he did know more than he was saying."

"What's his name?"

"Dmitry," he said clearing his throat. "He...he has a lot of resentment in his heart." He stuttered. "I 'spose it's partly my fault. He learned about love and loss quite young." He looked into his glass. "I had another son too. His name was Baker. He died with a bullet to his head."

"I'm sorry to hear that, sir. I didn't mean to make you relive the memories."

"No...it's been some time now. His mother was so over-protective and she still couldn't save him from himself. Dmitry was the oldest of the two."

"Did Baker and Dmitry have the same mother?"

"No. Baker's mother and me separated a long...long time ago. She was a mean woman. One of the meanest you'd ever meet, I promise you. I did allow Dmitry to go with Baker and his mother when she picked him up some-times, but Dmitry always seemed detached when he came back. It would take weeks for Dmitry to get back to normal. Now Baker was another conversation all together."

"What was Baker's mother's name?"

Estelle Hightower," he smiled reminiscing, "but I called her Penny. She was always so tight when it came to our budget. If there was a bargain to be gained, Estelle would find it down to the Penny." He chuckled at his own humor.

"Did you say, Penny?"

"Yes, son. Why?"

"'Cause the name sounds familiar. *Really* familiar."

"Yeah well she was something else. I never married her, I was going to because of Baker and I had just started my ministry here at the church. I wanted to set an example for my sons. But when Baker died, my reason to be with her died along with him. Baker was a disappointment to Penny. I've never seen a woman so obsessed with having a baby girl. That's all she wanted...truly. A daughter. But the way

Baker was born scarred any chances of her having another. I think she resented it. We didn't have no health care in them days and the doctor ripped up her womb to pull Baker out. He was a big baby. But I think God was saving the world by making her barren. Penny is pure evil. Now I don't believe in astrology, but there's something to be said about that Gemini sign. She could make you think she loved you one minute and you'd see the hate the next."

"Thank you so much, Pastor Robinson. Can I have your son's number?"

"Sure." He said grabbing a pen from inside his suit jacket pocket along with a small pad that he used to write down the notes from his sermons. "And, son, be careful. Some folks don't like people digging up the earth."

"I'll be fine."

"I hope so."

"Sir, do you mind if I return here if I have any more questions? As I mentioned on the phone, this case is really important to me and a few others who haven't given up the hope to at least find Gabriella's body."

"You're welcome anytime."

Terrell got up to leave, drank the milk and frowned. It was sour. At first he thought it was spoiled until he remembered the reverend downed it like it was fresh off the milk truck.

Picking up the gallon to examine it Terrell said, "This is past its due date sir. You have to throw it away or you'll get sick."

"There's nothin' wrong with this milk," he said slowly. "It's an acquired taste. Some people adopt evil tastes in life; I just like old milk,"

Terrell didn't know what the hell the pastor meant

but he left with more information than he knew what to do with. And, on top of that he left with a whole lot of mystery.

RECOLLECTION

Terrell was surprised that Dmitry was prompt, because when he made it to Busboy and Poets, a restaurant on 14th street in Washington D.C., he was already into his second drink, all on Terrell's dime. Terrell knew it was Dmitry the moment he saw him, because he looked strikingly like his father and was looking around the restaurant when he walked through the door.

"Thanks for meeting me, Terrell said scooting in a seat across from him. He extended his hand but Dmitry didn't take it.

His face was stern and silver hairs were sprinkled throughout his head. He figured he was about forty and he was dressed simply in a pair of blue jeans and a white t-shirt. He didn't look like he'd be living in Simple City.

"I already had two drinks, thank you," Dmitry said making it known that Terrell was paying for them, not him. "You got my money?"

"Yes. But before I give you anything, I need to see what you know. So talk."

Dmitry placed his right arm up on the bench behind him and twirled the drink in his cup with his straw. Something Terrell had seen the reverend do.

"Sometimes, I use to go with my brother Baker on weekends and Penny, his mother, didn't mind. I remember thinking she was so cool, you know, to let me come with her even though I wasn't her child. At first we'd *just* go to her house, but after while, she started taking us to work with her."

"Where did she work?"

Dmitry looked up at Terrell with horror in his eyes and Terrell was immediately uncomfortable. He looked around the restaurant and when he was sure no one was watching he said, "I can never tell you that. What I will say is, on the outside it looked like one thing, but when you went on the inside it was something totally different. I called it 'The Place'."

"You gotta tell me the name at least."

"I don't gotta tell you shit!" He yelled with an attitude, "all I gotta do is survive." He stared him down coldly. "But...downstairs there was this girl, Gabriella, the one you asked me about on the phone. She was as young as the rest of them, but in charge. I guess you could say she was the one keeping the other kids together. But she was so thin," he said shaking his head. "I...I can't understand some things about life you know? Like...how can people be so fuckin' cruel. To kids at that.

"But even though she wasn't being taken care of, she was alive with life. To me she was older than her years and had a spirit about her nobody else had. I've never met a person like her and still haven't to this day." He said shaking his head. "I think I was like sixteen or seventeen and she was 'bout nine or ten back then but I really can't remember."

"Did you say anything to Penny about the kids you saw? And the fact that they weren't eating?"

"No. I wasn't supposed to be down there," he said softly, "I wasn't supposed to know about any of that. She made it clear to us the moment we got there that downstairs was off limits. Upstairs and downstairs were like two different worlds. But me and my brother Baker was kids, so we roamed around and we got into shit. And on the weekends I wasn't with my brother, he'd actually stayed with Penny there sometimes when she had night-shifts, and that's when he found the world downstairs and told me about it."

"Look...when you were there, do you remember someone by the name of Yvonna?"

He looked directly into his eyes and said, "Yes. Gabriella and Yvonna were very close. Best friends I think. When Gabriella used to find rats to eat, she'd share them with Yvonna first and the others second."

"Rats?!" Terrell screamed. "How would children know to eat them let alone cook 'em?"

"You'd be surprised at what you would learn to do if you was hungry. They'd make little barnyard fires in the back of the area and cook their food off of makeshift pans. Since the people who kept the place often gave them old milk, they'd make cheese with it using the cloth from their dresses. They knew how to survive."

Terrell couldn't help but remember the old milk the reverend drank as if it were nothing.

"The point is, Gabriella cared for all the kids. When they were hungry, it was her who snuck into the alley, to bring in thrown out food from the dumpster of the restaurant that was across the street. And if she couldn't get some food, she'd kill another rat."

"I wonder why she didn't tell someone."

"It's not that easy," he said irritated with Terrell. "They would threaten to hurt these kids, and Gabriella had every reason to believe that they would."

"Please continue."

"Well when the restaurant closed, and the garbage wasn't as plentiful anymore, I decided to steal my father's car and meet her around the back of the place. He didn't even know I could drive but I'd been stealing his car for two years by then. I could only do it on Sundays though because he'd be in church all day with no use for his car.

"Anyway, when I would pick her up, I'd bring her to the church after the members would bring over their cooked dishes. My father's church always made large dinners on Sundays so the food she'd take would be enough to last the rest of the kids for a week."

"How many kids were there?"

"They'd come and go. But for the most part, there appeared to be about ten downstairs and fifteen upstairs at any given time. The ones upstairs were always so neat and clean but the ones downstairs were a different story. I got the impression that the ones downstairs weren't wanted, for whatever reason. I think they wouldn't conform. They were the rebellious ones."

"Why didn't you just tell your father?"

Dmitry laminated for a few seconds and said, "Because Gabriella, asked me not to. I was too young to understand what was happening so I respected her wishes. An even now, I still don't understand why I never told, I was real naïve." He swallowed hard. "The church thing worked and she was never supposed to get caught, but eventually she did. Luckily for Gabriella my father ended up liking her and they had her back every Sunday. Things were going good until...until..."

His pause irritated Terrell, as he felt closer to knowing

all of the things he ever wanted to know.

"Until Penny found out, that we'd been downstairs."

"How did it happen?"

"After I saw what kind of person Penny was, I didn't want to be around her, so I would go to see Gabriella on my own without staying over Penny's for the weekend. I wasn't worried about Penny finding out I was bringing Gabriella because she shied away from the church. She pretended to be Christian and would even talk to the Lord, but it was as if something was in it for her, but that was the extent of her religion.

"Anyway, Gabriella could've escaped *The Place* because anyone of the congregation members would've loved to have her. She was cool that way." He smiled for the first time since their meeting. "But there was a darker side to Gabriella. She would sometimes get into it with the adults if they hurt one of the other kids too badly. She set fires to their cars. Snuck upstairs and peed in their food, that kind of stuff. Those kids were her family. They would beat her but after awhile, it just didn't work. She stopped being afraid."

"What about the parents? Where were they?"

"I don't think she had one. Any of them. They seemed to be dumped off or...born there."

"Born there?"

"Yes," he said looking around again, "sometimes there were babies in there too. They got a little more attention than the others but not much. I remember seeing a young girl, who was about thirteen years old, breast-feeding two babies that weren't even hers. Her baby had been taken away from her recently but a new one had been born and placed downstairs in her care. And because her young body still produced milk, she had it to feed the babies. But when the babies were well enough, they were taken too.

And if there wasn't a baby to drink the milk, the baby-less mother would nurse the older kids to prevent them from starving." A tear dropped down Dmitry's face. Terrell was stunned silent.

"I...I can't imagine you witnessing something so violent and holding it all on yourself."

"Where's my money?" Dmitry asked as if someone had flipped a switch. "I'm not tellin' you nothin' else 'till you give me my money."

Terrell was put off by his change in mood at first but gave him the three hundred dollars that he asked for over the phone. "Why didn't you tell the police?"

"We were going to. Me and my brother. That's when Penny found out. I remember being scared at first but Baker, man...he was real strong. He said if we didn't tell someone, God wouldn't protect us if we needed help," he smiled again tucking the money into his pocket.

"But your father told me he killed himself. How could a kid so strong commit suicide?"

"That's a lie." Dmitry spat. "Don't ever fuckin' say that lie in my presence again!"

"Well...what did happen?"

"Penny found out that we was going downstairs, when one day she came to one of the rooms upstairs that we was supposed to be in and we weren't there. We were downstairs as usual. But Baker made a mistake and left a letter in his dresser drawer that he was planning to give his teacher the next day at school. It listed everything he saw downstairs and he'd even counted all the kids that were present.

"When Penny found the letter, she started keeping my brother out of school and started medicating him. She claimed he was sick but Baker had always been in good health. She said he was seeing people and hearing things but I'm not surprised, she kept him doped up! Any one of us would've lost our minds!

"I would tell my father that I believed something was wrong with Penny's story about Baker being sick, but he was so caught up in the church responsibilities that he didn't listen. The only reason I didn't tell him the exact details was because I was worried about my brother's life. My father didn't seem strong enough to take my word as fact, and investigate silently and I knew he'd tell Penny and that would further put my brother in danger.

"I remember sneaking my father's car to see Baker one Sunday, when Penny wasn't there. She used to run out all the time and leave him alone. Anyway, she had him so drugged up that he was like a zombie. He didn't even know who I was. The next day, he was dead. Everybody believed her story that he killed himself because Penny was well liked. But I never bought the story that he shot himself in the head one bit. He was too much in love with life.

"Well...what about Gabriella?"

"Luckily Penny still didn't know about me taking her out of 'The Place' on Sundays. So, I was still able to pick her up once a week through the crawl space she created to come and go. But one day one of the other kids over-heard Penny's plan to kill Gabriella because she was much stronger than they were. The plan was to murder Gabriella the following day. So we knew we had to move quickly. I picked up Gabriella the next morning, gave her some money I had stolen from the collection plate at church, and dropped her off at the public train station. That was the last I *saw* of her.

"So...so...you...knew where she went?" he paused as he looked at him with hopeful eyes. "All this time people thought she was probably..."

"She was very much alive last I saw her."

"But, so many people were looking for her, and could never find her. How is it possible for a child to disappear off the face of the earth?"

"That's where the story is lost for me. Six months after she left, she wrote me a letter telling me how much she appreciated my help and that she was okay. It was the last time I ever heard from her."

Terrell exhaled having felt like he had gotten so close, only to be so far away. His head dropped in defeat. "But my father...I'm sure he knows."

Terrell looked up from the table and said, "How do you know?"

"I'm not sure, but something tells me she told him more than she let on. They were really close and he cared about her. He even has a non-profit organization to feed the children in her name. I don't think he'd ever tell you anything, but I'm sure that at some point, when she left, she got in contact with him and told him she was okay. My father had a reward for any information leading to her whereabouts, but after awhile, it just went away. I asked him what made him cancel the reward and he said he had to move on with his life. But he was passionate about finding her before then so it didn't make much sense."

"Wow!" he said shaking his head. The love for the sour milk made so much sense to him now. "And what about Yvonna? Do you know what happened to her during the time she was in there?"

"No, but I do remember she was very clingy to Gabriella. She was the one person out of the group who looked up to her. But it wouldn't take them long to forget her. Most of them were drugged up half the time. They would give 'em the drugs in tea. Hot tea. I remember going back to 'The Place', a few days after Gabriella left to give them some food, and all of a sudden, the girl name Yvonna didn't recognize me anymore. And when I asked her about Gabriella, she didn't remember her name either. A few days later I went back again, and the crawl space was boarded up." Terrell looked at Dmitry and smiled.

"You know, your father told me you weren't approachable."

"I needed to get this off my chest. It's been weighing on me." He smiled. "Now I can move on with my life. Anyway all my father cared about was Gabriella at one point. I think he loved her more than he did his own kids. He could've protected Baker from Penny, but he didn't."

"Well thank you, man. This helped me out a lot."

Later on that day, Dmitry was run off of the side of the road and killed. No one saw a thing.

BODILY SACRIFICE

Swoopes was in bed with Newbie when Crystal walked quietly into the room. She stayed the night out hoping Swoopes would beg her to come home, but he never did. She couldn't believe he had the nerve to bring another female in the house that was in her name. She had met Swoopes on a prison pen pal site and fell head over heels in love with him. But Swoopes never loved her and barely liked her. He only used her to put the house and the car in her name, but beyond that, she wasn't worth shit.

A tear fell down her pretty brown round face when she saw the girl, who looked ten years younger, lying in her man's arms. Thirty-two year old Crystal could work hard to be pretty, but young, she would never be again. Newbie draped her leg across Swoopes and nestled her head comfortably in the center of his chest. They both were naked and fast asleep.

"Swoopes!" Crystal yelled dropping her purse to the floor. "What the fuck is goin' on in here?"

Newbie woke up and draped the white sheet over her naked body but Swoopes yanked them away. "What the fuck it look like? We sleepin'."

Crystal lunged after Newbie and at first Swoopes didn't stop her. He was tired of Crystal complaining about his crew members being over all the time and he was tired of her not keeping house.

"Get off of me!" Newbie yelled swinging wild arms at her. "Get away!"

Crystal was beating the naked girl so badly it wasn't funny. So Swoopes, with one hand, hoisted her off of Newbie. When she swung and hit him by mistake, he backhanded her and she fell to the floor.

Crystal looked up at him with pity on her face. "I don't understand. Why are you doin' this to me?"

Swoopes slid on his boxers and white t-shirt and slipped on his flip flops and Newbie got dressed too. When he was done he grabbed his gun and tucked it in his boxers under his shirt. Newbie was right behind him like a shadow. He swaggered into the living room and almost forgot he had Chavis clean the house because it was so neat.

The moment he sat in his recliner, Chavis handed him a breakfast sandwich and coffee and Swoopes shook his head. He split it and two and gave the other half to Newbie. Swoopes lost all respect for Chavis when he saw he was still there.

Growl and Cane slid through the front door, with an update on their connect when they looked up and saw Crystal coming out of the room holding her face. Seeing Newbie still there, they already knew if something hadn't kicked off, it was about to.

"We talked to the white boy," Cane said looking at Growl, "And he ain't gonna budge on that three week timeframe. He said he has some other clients and can't fuck with it any earlier than that."

"Bet...I guess we gonna start lookin' for somebody else."

"You want us to cancel?" Growl asked.

"Naw...we'll let the clock tick until we can find somebody else."

"Can you fuckin' talk to me please?" Crystal asked interrupting their meeting.

"Want me to get her outta here?" Growl asked looking at Crystal.

"What? You gonna treat me like this ain't even my house, too?" Crystal cried. "Is that what you gonna do? Afta all the meals I made for you?" Growl ignored her and waited for Swoopes' response. He wasn't into sympathy.

"Naw. She cool. But if she wanna stay here, she gonna have to get with the new program." Newbie sat at Swoopes foot like a dog. She didn't say much and that's one of the reasons he liked her.

"Well I'm not gonna go for it!" Crystal cried. "This my house and all ya'll mothafuckas gotta leave!"

"Bitch, I pay the bills here! You don't do shit but lay around and keep a fucked up house. That's why I got this young thing right here. Maybe your old ass ain't worth what you use to be. Matta fact," he said standing up, "I want you outta here." He grabbed her by her hair and pulled her toward the door. She dropped to the floor to make it harder for him to move her.

"Stop!" she pleaded. "I don't wanna leave! Don't make me go."

"Well it's too late, bitch!" He continued as the veins in his muscular arms bulged as he pulled.

"Please!" She screamed. "I'll do anything. Don't put me out."

He released her and watched her thump onto the floor. "Get up!" he told her. Swoopes seemed to be enjoying the scene.

Crystal rose and said, "Yes?"

"If you said you'd do anything, I want you to fuck one of my men."

"What? I...I don't understand."

"Newbie!" He screamed with his eye still remaining on Crystal.

"Yes, God."

"I want you to fuck one of my men." His eyes never left Crystal's.

"Which one, God?"

"You see?" Swoopes said to Crystal. "No questions asked. If you can't have that same spirit, then I don't need you."

Crystal had never been more humiliated in all her life. She gave up everything for him, including custody of her two little girls. All because Swoopes seemed to have a hatred toward kids.

"Crystal," he said in her face. "I want you to fuck one of my men."

"Which one?" Crystal said softly.

"I can't hear you." Swoopes said turning his head as he normally did so that his ear was close to her mouth.

"Which one, God?"

Swoopes looked around the room. Cane, Growl and Chavis were all present. "Which one of ya'll gonna fuck my girl?"

"Come on, man, this is gettin' stupid," Cane said. "Ain't nobody in this room gonna fuck your girl."

"What...ya'll scared?" he asked looking between Growl and Cane.

"I can't do it either," Growl told him.

Thinking this was his moment to win Swoopes' favor and get out of the kitchen; Chavis took off the apron and said, "I'll do it."

Swoopes looked at him and then at Crystal and said, "There you go. Chavis will fuck you."

"Pleeeassssse, Swoopes. I don't wanna do this. My body is only for you."

"Either you do it, or you dropped. It's as simple as that."

With her head hung low, she and Chavis went into the room and closed the door. Cane leaned against the wall in frustration and Growl sat on the sofa and started playing one of the video games. They knew it did no good in saying anything to Swoopes. He was beyond reproach. Swoopes flopped down on his recliner and eyed the closed door as if he could see straight through the wood.

Five minutes later, Crystal came out of the bedroom sobbing before she ran into the bathroom. The sounds of her throwing up could be heard in the living room. Chavis entered the living room, adjusting his belt through the final hole.

But the moment his feet passed the bedroom's threshold, Swoopes lifted his gun and shot him in the head. No one saw it coming so Growl jumped off of the sofa, and grabbed his heat while Cane watched Chavis' body hit the floor.

"I ain't neva like his ass anyway," he said softly putting his gun down beside him.

"What's goin' on, cuzo?" Cane asked pacing the floor. He had one hand on his head and the other on his waist. "Why you so reckless all of a sudden? What happened to you in prison, man?"

"I need to find this bitch, like yesterday, and shit ain't movin' fast enough for me. Until I do, to be honest, Cane," he said looking at him, "I can't be liable for what I might do." The silent threat was geared at all of them.

"Man, if findin' her will get you back to normal, on my life, I'ma help you wit' this bitch."

"Good. For now, get rid of that dead nigga."

HATEFUL HUSBANDS

Yvonna was tied up to a wooden chair looking at Avante. She couldn't get over how bad he let the house go. Trash was everywhere and the smell of rotten food lingered throughout the hallways. Yvonna had a way of making the sanest take a walk on the insane side.

"Avante, what are you doing?" she asked calmly. "You're not gonna get away with kidnapping me. This is crazy."

"You talk about crazy?" he laughed. "Yeah right." Avante who once was clean-shaven sported a long weird grungy beard. The jeans he was wearing were too big, and he looked as if he'd been rolling around in dirt for three days.

Ever since his wife Treyana was murdered, he fell hard. And although the police officers told him that it was Cream, his ex lover, who murdered her, Avante believed Yvonna was responsible. Despite them finding Cream's fingerprints on the electrical panel Treyana was stuffed in. Things got worse when Cream's hand was found, without her body.

"What are you gonna do, Avante? Can you at least talk to me?"

Avante worked diligently on setting up a video camera, directly across from her. He seemed preoccupied by his own mind. Eventually he turned around, shot her an evil glare and walked over to her. "You have taken everything from me! You even had everything to do with why Cream and I didn't get married, then you killed Treyana and now my kids are in Maryland's foster care system. I have nothing left, but the testimony that you *will* give today. And if you don't tell them everything you've done, I'm gonna kill you." He said going back to the video camera set up. "It will be my pleasure."

"This is why you don't leave witnesses and you finish what you start," Gabriella said sitting on the floor beside Yvonna. "Even if you do admit to murdering Treyana, he's not gonna let you go. I hope you know that shit."

"So what am I gonna do?" She whispered, not wanting to alert Avante that all the stories about her being crazy were true. "He has me tied up to this chair with my arms behind my back. I can't fuckin' move."

"Oh...so now you need my help."

"I need to get out of this," Yvonna said.

"Do you now know the importance of finishing what you started? Is it clear to you now that some people would rather see you covered in dirt, than happy?"

"Yes."

"So what do we do when we get out of here?"

"We finish." She said looking at Avante's back.

"Finish what?" Gabriella persisted.

"Avante."

Yvonna looked at Avante and suddenly became angry. Sure she was the one who murdered Treyana, and framed Cream. But in her mind she did him a favor. After all, she fucked her dead boyfriend Bilal, had twin boys by him, and passed them off as Avante's kids.

"Good...so this is what we're going to do, we're going to play on his weakness."

"What is his weakness and how is that going to get me outta here?"

"Look at him, Yvonna. He's lonely. He thinks he's doing all of this to avenge his wife's death. But what he's really doing this for is to hide his shame. He's afraid to be alone. Just like most men, he's weak. But make him think he needs you."

"He's not gonna buy it."

"Make him buy it," Gabriella said, standing behind the chair and whispering into her ear, "Make him see that you can be everything to him that he needs. Look around, you can tell he barely leaves this roach infested house. I bet the most adventure he had in two years was snatching you out the back door of CVS and bringing you here. Make him see he needs you as much as you need him. That's always been your power...to seduce. Use it!"

Gabriella disappeared and Yvonna got into character.

"Avante," she said his name softly and slowly. He ignored her. "Avante, please, can we talk?"

Avante looked in her direction but over her. She was irritating him and that made him mad. "What?" he said turning around, fiddling with the TV again.

"I'm sorry." She said, but it wasn't good enough and she knew it. If she wanted his attention she had to hit harder. "I'm sorry for murdering your wife."

Now those words had Avante's *full* attention. He stopped what he was doing and walked slowly toward her. It was the first confirmation he had that he'd been right all along. Only if the world was there to witness it.

"I know you did it, bitch! But why? Why would you do something like that? You destroyed a family. Who does that kind of shit?"

"A sick person. I'm sick, Avante. And I'm sorry."

In order to do a good job at seduction, she had to imagine him as he was before. Prior to falling off, Avante's smooth chocolate skin, and chiseled features reminded everyone of the singer/actor Tyrese. She needed that mental picture instead of the hunk of shit that stood before her.

"But she didn't deserve you, Avante. She never did." Her voice was seductive.

"My wife loved me!" he yelled pointing to himself. "What are you talkin' about?" Spit escaped his mouth and he resembled a wild animal off a leash. "We had a life! We had a home...and you took that away from us! I knew the moment I laid eyes on you at me and Cream's engagement party that you were trouble. I just couldn't convince the people around me that it was true." Tears flowed from his eyes and Yvonna was disgusted. *What country do they breed these weak ass niggas in?*

"Avante, look at you."

"Fuck you mean?" he said quickly wiping the tears from his face. He had so much hair around his mouth, it resembled a dry pussy.

"Just what I said. Take a good look at yourself." He briefly looked himself over but he couldn't understand what she meant. "You're crying over a woman who passed off another man's kids as yours." Avante slapped her so hard, her lips cracked but she smiled. Pain was nothing to her. Mentally she could escape her body while others would fold under pressure. "The twin boys are not yours," Yvonna said again. And again he slapped her and her face turned right. But she looked at him again and said, "They weren't your sons. They never will be."

This time he punched her in the stomach and her head dropped forward. Air violently exited her body and she had to admit, she felt that shit. Slaps and punches she could take, but punches to the gut were another story. It was her weakness.

Raising her head she said, "The kids were not yours." She wanted him to take the anger out on her because she knew that's what he really wanted. To make the person responsible for killing his wife feel the pain he did. Avante, still angry, stood over her and wrapped his hands around her throat. She knew he enjoyed inflicting pain while having sex, so choking Yvonna brought her closer to freedom.

But something went wrong, he was tightening his grip and he had appeared to black out. If he continued with the pressure he was placing on her, she wouldn't make it. She tried to talk to him but words weren't coming from her mouth. What was she going to do? She'd tested the limits and now there was hell to pay.

As a last resort, she used her strength to mouth the words, "She didn't deserve you."

At first Avante was unresponsive and more interested in bringing her closer to death. Sweat fell off of his face and entered her eyes, momentarily blinding her.

But again she mouthed, "She didn't deserve you," although she was feeling lighter.

This time he lessened his grip and this allowed her to get some air, "She didn't deserve you." She said a little more audible. "She never did."

Now he was crying so hard, it was difficult to watch. He unfettered his hold and collapsed to the floor. Yvonna would've given anything to be able to rub her neck but she was still tied up.

Coughing a few times to clear her passageway she

said, "She wasn't right for you, Avante." She would repeat it as many times as necessary, because the statement worked. And...saying anything else could result in her getting choked out again. "You deserve a woman who can handle you. One who can be there for you like you need her to be."

Avante stopped sobbing like a three year old for a fleeting moment and said, "You don't even know me."

"Avante I know everything about you. How do you think I was able to get Treyana back in your good graces? I knew what dress to tell her to wear the night of you and Cream's engagement party to get your attention. I knew what you wanted from her mentally, so I convinced her to go back to night school. I imagined how soft you'd like her skin to feel while making love, and I taught her what scented lotions to use, and how to respond to your touch."

His eyes widened and she had him mesmerized. "How did you know all of them things?"

"I knew what you wanted because that woman you wanted was me."

Now the tables were turned and she was in control. He was caught in her web, and like a fly trying to get out, it was a wrap. He could do nothing but submit.

"I use to fantasize about you all the time, Avante. That's why the moment you took me from CVS, initially I wasn't scared. I was just happy to be in your presence. Happy that you had your hands on me and happy to have your attention, no matter what the reason."

Avante's eyes widened and he hung on to her every word like a grown bitch listening attentively to Santa Claus. "Release me, Avante. Let me make love to you."

"No! You just trying to escape."

"I understand why you would feel that way, based on

113

what you think you know about me, but you have to remember, people make things up to sell papers. And a lot of women are jealous of me. Give me a chance and forge your own opinions about my motives. Because at the end of the day I'm still a woman, and I still have needs. Will you supply some of them for me?"

Avante stood up and Yvonna could see his dick harden. This was the response she needed. She had convinced a man who just twenty minutes earlier wanted to kill her, to submit to her spell.

"How I know you not playing games?"

"You don't. But you are a man, Avante, look into my eyes. Does it seem like I'm playing games with you? You have the upper hand. Not me."

Five seconds later he was releasing the ropes from her wrists until she said, "No...don't release the ropes fully."

"Why not?"

"I want you to feel comfortable. I want to make love to you with you knowing that all I want is you. Let my hands stay in front of me, with the rope tied around my wrists. Just tie it wide enough apart so I can still touch you. And remove the rope from my feet, so I can let you inside of me. This way you're still in control."

Avante hurriedly removed her pants and tied the rope around her wrists the way she'd asked.

"You know I'm just getting home don't you? From the institution?"

"Yes," he said undressing. His dingy pants hung at his ankles. The way he smelled, she knew there was no way on earth she was fucking Monkey Butt.

"One of the things I missed when I was in was getting my pussy licked. I use to finger my clit and pretend it was a warm tongue. Could you kiss it for me?"

Avante eagerly spread her legs apart. And as if he was eating ice-cold watermelon on a hot summer afternoon, he dived into her wetness. She couldn't lie; his pussy eating skills were top notch. Who knew the caveman had it in him? Avante rolled his tongue around her clit giving it a few light flicks every now and again. Normally mixing business with pleasure was a no-no, but as far as she was concerned, because of the drama he'd caused, he owed her a good pussy lick.

"That's it, Avante. Eat that shit. Ummmm Mmmmmmm," She moaned. "Move that tongue around like that," Yvonna coached as she widened her legs.

Her orgasm was coming on so she moved her hips closer to his lips and oozed her love oil all over his face. But instead of letting him know, she pretended to be 'not quite there'. Instead she grabbed the rope that was around her wrists, and pulled it tightly apart. And with Avante between her legs, she quickly wrapped the rope around his throat once, and then twice, pulling both ways tightly.

He was taken off guard as he reached up for her neck. His weight pushed them back in the chair and they toppled to the floor. But Yvonna was as strong as an ox, having killed before. She gripped the rope tighter and tighter until he was barely fighting. And even when she saw his tongue hang from the side of his mouth, and his eyes roll up in his head, she continued to tighten the rope.

When she was sure he was no longer a burden, she pushed him off of her, untied herself, and got dressed.

Before she left she wiped the place down to remove her fingerprints. Now she had to get out. Luckily for her, Bricks was calling. And she figured it was high time they got reacquainted.

MIND READER

Yvonna sat across from Jona for the first time in a long time. There were a ton of papers on her desk and she trifled through them, pretending to be busier than she actually was. Yvonna's presence frightened her, no matter how hard she tried to hide it. While Yvonna basked in the fact that she was scared of her, she noticed something that bothered her. A picture of Jona and Terrell sat proudly on her desk, and was faced in Yvonna's direction.

"So you fuckin' my ex?" Yvonna started. "Let's talk about it."

"What are you talking about now, Yvonna?"

"The bitch thinks she's so slick," Gabriella said.

Yvonna laughed at Gabriella's comment but Jona being so self-conscious thought she was laughing at her. Terrell had broken her down so badly, there was nothing left of her.

"You know what I'm talking about, Jona. You have the picture faced me, so let's talk about what you wanna talk about. Terrell."

"What?" Jona said looking at their picture. "Oh...I'm sorry, I didn't even know that was right there."

"You're boring him aren't you?"

"Me and Terrell are perfectly happy," she lied.

"Doubt it." Yvonna laughed. "I bet you can't even suck a straw. A man like Terrell likes his dick sucked twenty four seven you know, that's how I roped his ass."

"What happened to your face, Yvonna?" Jona asked attempting to skip the subject. Yvonna had forgotten that Avante had bruised her face.

"Nothing...just a little rough sex." She giggled.

"Let's get down to business. I called Penny's house and she told me you hadn't been staying there for the past couple of days. You know this is a violation of your release."

Yvonna felt like choking Penny's fat neck ass out. Just yesterday she asked her had she ratted her out, and she told her no. Now she was finding out she lied.

"Well I been in and out, but for the most part, I've been staying wit' Penny."

"Well where are you *staying* for the other parts?" Jona asked in a condescending tone. "Since it's obvious you're going to do whatever you want to do."

"Look, Jona, sign them fuckin' papers on your desk, and let me get the fuck outta here. Because we both know you don't give a fuck about me gettin' better, and I don't give a fuck about you."

When she finished her statement, her phone rang.

"Hello." Yvonna crossed her jean-covered legs, and wiggled her shoe while irritating the hell out of Jona because she answered the phone. "Who's this?"

"Yvonna. What's up?"

When she heard his voice, the smile was removed from her face. Her eyes were looking in Jona's direction but her mind was on how the fuck did Swoopes get her cell phone number. He was proving to be more of a problem than she realized. She wasn't use to being the hunted.

"Yvonna, we're in a meeting and I demand that you respect it!" Jona said, like she had authority.

Yvonna gave her a look like, *'Bitch please'*, and rolled her eyes. "How did you get this number? This is a new phone number so you shouldn't have it."

"The same way I got your house number. You need to start asking the right questions, like why am I calling."

"Well what do you want? We already know we got a beef so let's handle it in the streets."

"I want you to meet me somewhere, so that we can put this all behind us. I wanna call a truce. So what you doin' tomorrow?"

"Swoopes, I ain't got time for this shit. If you wanna see me then see me. It's as simple as that."

"How old is your little girl?" he asked as if they were long lost friends. "Is she two or three? I followed her the other day to the mall, she was with some woman who looked like Shrek." He laughed at his own humor.

"Swoopes," Yvonna said getting up from her seat, "I understand why you want me. I get that, but if you fuck wit' my daughter, you gonna see a side of me I haven't shown you yet. And you already know what I can do. Oh yeah...how was the prison ass fuck I arranged for you? I heard he had you *wide* open."

"Bitch, I can't wait to get my hands on you!" She knew she struck a nerve. "But I'm gonna return the favor to that little bitch you gave birth to," he laughed, "I wonder how far her little asshole will stretch wit' my dick in it."

Yvonna knew then that she had to get her daughter from Penny's house. Her face felt extra warm to the touch and her temperature was boiling. "You gonna wish you never said that shit to me."

"We'll see 'bout that, Yvonna."

When he hung up she flopped down in her seat. She didn't want to be there but for now she didn't have a choice. She called Penny a few times but she didn't answer so she decided to leave a message.

"Penny, I'm gonna come pick up Delilah for a few days," she told her on the voicemail. "Can you please have her ready? Oh...and please be careful." She threw the phone in her lap.

"Sounds like you haven't been home a week, and already you're in trouble. What is it with you, Yvonna? Why does it seem like everywhere you go, drama follows?"

Yvonna walked up to the desk and said, "I'm about to take care of some things but let me tell you somethin' before I leave, I know what I am and I'm tired of people fuckin' wit' me because of it. Especially you," she laughed looking her over. "Look at you! You not even no real doctor. Your hair looks a mess...you got rings under your eyes, and you fuckin' wit' one of your patient's ex-men. So you're not about to waste any more of my time pretending to be something you're not. Now, I'ma walk outta here and show you the back of my ass, and if you fuck with me, by trying to get me locked back up, I'll let them see this," she said swiping the picture from her desk. "Cause I'm sure this breaks the patient doctor confidentiality thing."

Yvonna walked to the door and said, "And I'll come to my next appointments if I can, but if I can't I don't expect no problems either. Bye, bitch."

←——————————————————————→

After her appointment, Bricks men brought Yvonna

to his house. Yvonna sat in his living room waiting to hear the news he had for her. She hoped it had everything to do with Swoopes because after the threat he made on her daughter, he was becoming a pain in her ass. So either they were going to help her find him, or she was going to have to find him herself.

"You 'aight," Bricks asked when he saw the scars on her face.

"I had a long day." She said placing her hand on her scars. "How's the arm?"

"It's cool. Almost don't even feel it nomore," he said in a manly gruff. "Why you leave outta here like that last night? And why were you talking like you were somebody else?"

"Is that why you called me here?"

"No." He said softly. When he sat down, she got a whiff of his cologne and her stomach fluttered. Every time she got around him, she wanted him to hold her, but would feel soft if she said it.

"Your hair looks good, I like it short." He said bluntly.

"Thanks." Yvonna said trying not to blush.

"Where's Kendal? I don't have time for her shit today."

"I put Kendal and her mother out last night. I don't feel like that shit 'round here no more."

"Oh..." Yvonna said. "I thought that would never happen."

"Well it's obvious you don't know me."

Yvonna swallowed hard and said, "I guess not."

"Sorry I went on you the way I did on the phone earlier, but a lot of shit been goin' on since you left last night."

"Like what?" Yvonna said now standing in the living room.

"Some nigga ran up in my cousin's girl's house, and killed her. Her daughter was home at the time and everything."

Yvonna felt sweat forming on her forehead and had to sit back down due to feeling dizzy. I mean, how many women get murdered in front of their daughter's every day? It had to be the same one she killed.

"Oh...for real? Where did it happen?"

"On my block. My little cousin said the nigga came through the front door but we know that ain't happen. We had too many people on guard. We think he came through the back door."

"So do you think it had something to do with Swoopes?"

"I'm not sure. My little cousin Tracy described this dealer named, Quest. So we took care of him last night. I just hope it was the right man."

Yvonna thought she should've felt bad that someone else got killed for something she did, but she didn't. "Oh...uh, how is your little cousin?"

"She in the room," he said pointing to Kendal's door. "She seems to be handlin' it 'aight."

"Who in the room?" Yvonna asked standing up.

"My little cousin. Why?" Bricks asked.

Yvonna hoped she didn't come out of the room and identify her as the one who really killed her mother.

"You see, that's why you don't leave no witnesses," Gabriella said sitting next to Bricks. "And did I tell you? He's cute."

"Shut up!" Yvonna yelled.

"You aight, shawty?" Bricks asked wondering what caused her to yell.

"Oh...yeah...I'm fine," she said looking at Gabriella. "What were you saying?"

"Normally I don't like your picks," Gabriella inter-rupted, making it hard for her to focus on Bricks, "but he's my speed. I think we gonna keep him."

The fact that she was anywhere near him caused Yvonna stress.

"I said are you 'aight?" Bricks repeated.

"I'm good, Bricks. I'm just sorry to hear about what happened to your little cousin."

"It's foul, but to be honest, Pam's hoe ass had it comin'. She stayed runnin' behind nigga afta nigga. That shit was bound to catch up wit' her. I was just fucked up that my lil cousin was there to see that shit."

"So what's up wit' Swoopes?" Yvonna asked skipping the subject. "Because today he threatened my daughter and I need that handled."

"I just got in touch with Mom's again today."

"Your mother?"

"No...the dude we went to see." He said looking at her like she was crazy. "He gave me some more information on them peoples that may help us. He's expectin' a big drop in three weeks at a spot in D.C. Some cats coming up from New York 'spose to give him some wet. Now we know exactly where they meetin' spot is."

"So he fuck wit' boat now?"

"Yeah, Mom's said he done fucked over so many niggas before he went in the Iron City, that he had to switch up. He knew he wasn't gettin' no more coke money when he got home. That's why he lost his eye and fingers. That nigga's sour."

"Look, I don't know if we can wait for three weeks."

"Then I suggest you go get your kid and find a new place to hide 'cause this dude don't hang in one place for too long. He's like a ghost. If you want," he paused, "ya'll could stay here wit' me 'til this shit blow over. I got plenty of space."

"No thanks, I got some place to stay."

Yvonna could catch the disappointment in his eyes and she wondered what it meant. Did he *really* want her to stay with him?

"That's up to you," he said like he didn't give a fuck, "but you should tell me where you're stayin'. I can have some people check up on you from time to time to make sure you 'aight."

"I really don't want anybody knowing where I'll be."

"So you don't trust me?"

"I'm not sayin' all that. I'm just sayin', the less people who know where I am the better."

"Listen," Bricks said turning his body around to look her in her eyes, "I'm glad you independent and shit, but this dude not gonna stop 'till he gets his hands on you. I'm not sure what you did to him, but it's enough to send him over the edge. Now the good thing about it is you got me on your side 'cause he put me in it. So take advantage of it and let me protect you." He paused but continued to stare into her eyes. "Now give me the address. I'ma make sure you 'aight."

Yvonna was shocked. Here another man was caring for her and she didn't know why. She was crazy, violent and selfish, yet for some reason, those exact traits appeared to draw men closer to her. She was use to people helping her because she held some deep dark secret over their head, but with Bricks it was different. He was protecting her because he wanted to.

Yvonna thought about it for a minute and said, "I'm stayin' over Ming's. But I'd appreciate if you kept it to yourself."

"I ain't tellin' nobody," he said handing her a pen and paper, "just write the address down so I can have it."

For a moment Bricks stared at Yvonna with his sexy grey eyes and it was unnerving. "What you lookin' at?"

She asked turning away.

"That mole on your ear," he said as if he was making some new discovery. "I never saw it before."

"Bricks please," she said embarrassed. "Don't act like you notice anything about me."

"You got two moles on your elbow and one on your right thigh. I notice everything."

"What? How do you know I have a mole on my thigh?"

"I saw it when you was downstairs. After Kendal spilled the grits on you."

Yvonna blushed. "How you remember that?"

"I notice a lot of things about people."

"People or just me?"

"People," he said clearing his throat.

"Oh," She said thoroughly embarrassed, "listen, if Mom's knows so much," Yvonna continued writing down Ming's address, "and wants Swoopes for his own reasons too, how come he don't just go kill him himself? You don't find that a little suspect?"

"I don't know what his angle is. I do know we've dealt in business wit' him in the past and those times he was legit. We just gonna have to take it for what it is."

While they were talking his little cousin Tracy came running into the living room. "Uncle Bricks, can I have a bowl of cereal?"

Tracy stopped short when she saw who was sitting with him. It was the same woman who killed her mother the night before.

"I know you big enough to go make it yourself, Tracy" he joked.

"Oh...okay," she said still eyeing Yvonna.

Yvonna didn't know if she was scared or what. So she waved at her and when Bricks wasn't looking, she put a finger over her lips wanting the little girl to keep her secret. The little girl nodded and smiled putting Yvonna at ease.

I'M A LITTLE TEAPOT

Thaddeus sat in the living room with the television blasted and he was consumed by the football game. Always a Dallas Cowboy fan, he was irritated that the Washington Redskins, a team he felt was weaker, was up by a touchdown. He tucked his hand halfway in the waist of his jeans, and allowed the beer he was drinking to rest comfortably on his large belly, which was covered by a soiled t-shirt. Although he used to be fine a century ago, years of daily alcohol abuse had taken its toll on him.

"Fuck! I can't believe they letting these sissies win!" He yelled before washing his mouth with ice-cold beer. "Baby, if they lose this game, I'ma owe Frank five hundred dollars!" He yelled at Penny who was cooking his dinner in the kitchen.

Penny walked into the living room and placed a bowl full of hot buttered popcorn on the table next to him. One of the ways she roped his ass was by catering to his every need. His wife, who thought they were still together, had stopped doing that the moment she discovered he slept with prostitutes and gave her herpes.

"Don't worry 'bout it, Thaddeus, you knows them boys ain't worth shit! They not gonna win." She bent over and kissed his lips and when she walked away, he slapped her large ass. She smiled believing she finally had it made by landing herself a man.

Delilah, who was uninvolved in the nonsense going on around her, sat on the floor with her brand new pink teacup set. For her guests she chose to invite her Cabbage Patch Kid Dolls, Aiden Luis and Shayna Jacey, but it was the fourth place set, which was empty that held her attention.

"Some for you," she said holding the teacup up and pouring it into her imaginary friend's mouth, "dwink up." She continued in her high-pitched child's voice.

Irritated that his team was losing, Thaddeus' bum ass used the time to bother the child. "Why you always talkin' to people who ain't there?" he said guzzling his beer, "Your mama in there done bought you all them nice toys and you still talk to yourself! Don't make no damn sense! You just like that crazy bitch who gave birth to you."

Delilah looked at the man and frowned, she didn't like him and anyone who watched him walk into a room when she was present knew it. Because the moment he'd show his face, she'd have a tantrum.

But instead of sobbing, she continued to feed the imaginary friend, leaving the other dolls thirsty. When she felt the imaginary friend, whom she called Ra-Ra, had enough tea, she talked to her.

"No...don't say that! That's bad!" Delilah said to Ra-Ra. She looked at Thaddeus and shot him a glare so cold, her intentions were known. She hated him and even as a child the look couldn't be mistaken for anything else.

"That's not nice."

Thaddeus believing the child's imaginary friend was talking about him, got real indignant-like and for no reason whatsoever, got up and knocked the entire tea set over before flopping back down in his seat. Delilah was livid. Thaddeus smirked like the Grinch and turned his eyes back to the game. The moment he did Delilah threw a tea cup in his direction hitting him in the forehead. But before he could react, she screamed and kicked wildly.

"What happened to the chile?" Penny asked running from the kitchen picking her up.

"She knocked her toys down." He lied knowing the child couldn't verbalize fully what really the fuck happened. He starred at her with anger and rubbed his forehead. "What's wrong, Delilah? Tell me so Mommy can make it better."

Penny was out of pocket for telling the child to refer to her as mommy, but she didn't care. As far as she was concerned she'd taken care of the girl so long, that she was the mother and Yvonna was just a surrogate.

"Why's you cryin', chile?"

Delilah pointed to Thaddeus but Penny, pushed her little hand down and walked away. She knew he could be impatient when it came to kids and she wished it wasn't so. She loved Delilah being around and she wanted him to like it too.

"Mama's gonna get yous some ice cream. Would ya like that?"

Delilah smiled and just like that, for the moment anyway, forgot about Thaddeus and his inconsideration of her toys. While they were in the kitchen, the doorbell rang. Thaddeus bitterly waddled to the door and opened it. It was the first time he and Yvonna met, and she didn't like him already.

"What you want?" he said with a beer in hand.

"I'm Yvonna. Where's Penny," she asked looking at the full-bodied, robust man before her. His body stank of sweat and his stomach hung over the belt of his jeans. "I came to pick my daughter up."

"Come on in," he huffed. "Penny, Yvonna's here for Delilah." He seemed to be relieved that she was coming to get the baby and Yvonna wondered why.

Penny walked out of the kitchen and the way she looked at Yvonna would forever stay etched in Yvonna's mind. For the first time ever, Yvonna felt Penny hated her.

"I came to pick up Delilah for a few days," Yvonna said. "And to grab my clothes and car out front. I left you a voicemail. You didn't get it?" When Yvonna looked over at the machine she saw the light wasn't on and knew she'd gotten her message.

"No I didn't," she frowned, "I just got the machine since your doctor be callin' and leavin' messages and I don't know how to use it yet. Where yous taking her anyway?"

Yvonna didn't think she had to tell her old ass shit, since Delilah was her daughter, but she also knew she'd been caring for the child for two years and there was going to be some attachment.

"We're just going to Ming's. And then maybe to Chuck-E-Cheese," she said as she moved to take her daughter out of Penny's hands. This time Delilah didn't fight, and seemed to want to be held by her mother. "I'll call you when we're on our way back." Yvonna smiled at the baby and played with her hand.

"I's don't feel too good about this," Penny said looking at Delilah. "I's think it's too early."

"Well *yous* gonna have to get use to it," Yvonna said

mocking her broken English. "I wanted you to care for my baby until I came home, not forever, Penny."

"I knows it's your baby, Yvonna, but I's cares 'bout her too."

"Good for you," Yvonna smiled slyly, before walking downstairs.

She grabbed a few things while maintaining her physical hold of Delilah and went back upstairs. She was just about to leave when she remembered something.

"Penny, I thought you told me you didn't tell Jona I didn't stay here. In my appointment today, she said you told her I wasn't staying here."

"I's didn't tell her that. That's your business not mines," she scowled still angry.

Yvonna could've gone back and forth with Penny but she didn't. All Penny had to do was make a call and they would no doubt re-institutionalize her, and take her baby from her. It was bad enough that she didn't have the relationship with Delilah that a mother and daughter should have. If Delilah were taken away from her again, she'd lose the precious years necessary to build a solid bond. It was now or never for them.

But...Yvonna kept quiet and made mental notes to be weary of a woman she once respected and loved. That day marked the turning point of their relationship, and it would be a day Yvonna would never forget.

SECRET REASONS

After Yvonna picked up Delilah, she went to Ming's house but she wasn't home. Ming called five minutes later telling her she needed to see her right away. There was something in her voice that sounded frantic and it put Yvonna on edge.

Yvonna decided to meet her at *Ketchup*, a restaurant at the National Harbor near Washington, D.C. Their specialty was fries with different types of sauces for dipping, so she chose that while she waited. And she had the waiter seat her near the window so that Delilah could be entertained by the water people passing by on the boardwalk.

As she watched Delilah play with her food, her mind wondered. Here she was the brokest she'd ever been in her life, and she had a child. All the times she earned money in the name of revenge, when it came to earning cash for love, she was coming up short with ideas on how to do it. Running her hand across her baby girl's face she made a vow.

"I'm gonna do whatever I gotta do, to take care of you."
The baby cooed, and went on about playing with her food.
For now Delilah could care less if they were busted or rich.

Minutes later, Ming walked in front of the window,
saw them sitting inside and waved. She was fifteen minutes late and in pure disarray. When she walked inside,
she flopped her white Louis Vuitton bag on the table, a
large black duffle bag on the floor and hollered for any
waiter to come over to the table. Luckily the waiter she
caught was her own and she ordered two vodka martinis.

"I see you have Delilah," Ming smiled. Her hair was
scattered all over her head, and it was obvious that she'd
been crying. "Must be nice to finally make family with
your baby."

"What's up, Ming?" Yvonna asked as Delilah played
happily in her high chair. "You don't look too good."

"Ming needs your help." She drank both Martinis
when the waiter brought them to the table.

Yvonna seeing this as a chance to get some capital
eagerly said, "You got that, what is it?"

Ming threw the bag under the table, on top of it and
examined her surroundings. When she was sure no one
was watching, she opened it. Inside were six bags of pure
white cocaine. "What the fuck are you doing?" Yvonna
asked looking around. "Close that shit up! My baby's in
here!"

Ming sat the bag back on the floor and looked around
again. Yvonna got the impression that she wasn't used to
dealing with drugs because she was frazzled instead of
cool and calm.

"Ming needs you to go with Darcus to New York, and
drop this off. It's very important this favor. I'll give you the
address."

"Ming, I can't do that." She whispered leaning in closer. "I have Delilah now. The risk is too big." She said as if she didn't just kill a mothafucka earlier in the day. Murder was her thing but running drugs up 95 was another story.

"Please," she begged. "Ming has to be on plane by the morning for China. If I don't drop this off, it will cause much problems for me and my family."

"First off, why is Darcus going?"

"Because I trust him."

"But you've only known him for a couple of months."

"Ming says she trusts him and he has nothing to do with my asking for your help. Are you not Ming's friend?!" She yelled beating her fist on the table.

Delilah looked at her and slapped her hand. "Stop!" she said turning her attention back to her food.

Ming looked at the child and dropped her head. "Ming this shit is too crazy. Talk to me." She knew if Ming was asking for her help, she really needed her but this was too much. That explained the huge bank account although she hoped she wasn't putting illegal drug money in a legal banking account.

"How long have you been involved in this?"

"There are many things you don't know about Ming. I'll leave it at that."

"When does this have to be done?" Yvonna sighed.

"In two days."

"I can't, Ming. I have Delilah for two days." She said sitting back in her seat, touching Delilah's foot. "I haven't spent any time with her and I don't want her not to know me."

Ming sat back in her seat and cried. "Ming has done everything for you that you asked." Tears poured out of her eyes like Demi Moore in the movie Ghost. "Ming even helped you dispose of body and now you don't want to help me?"

Yvonna reached over the table, and grabbed Ming's tiny throat. When she had a good hold of it, she squeezed tightly. "Listen, bitch, if you ever say somethin' about that night again, I'll kill you. And if I'm not mistaken, you're the one who sucked and fucked his ass before I killed him with your shoe. So as far as I'm concerned, we're both guilty."

When she thought Ming understood, she released the grip. Ming stood up and appeared to be transformed. "If you knew Ming's family, you would not have put your hands on me." She grabbed her purse and duffle bag. "A friend who doesn't help another in need is no friend at all." She said wiping her finger across the air. "So as far as I'm concerned, you dead to me."

Ming stormed out the restaurant and Yvonna fell back into her seat watching her only source of income walk out the door with her.

"Mam, can I get you something else?" The waiter asked. Yvonna's mind had wandered. "Mam. Are you okay?" He asked politely.

"Oh...yes, can you please bring me a strawberry daiquiri?"

"No problem," the kind waiter said.

Her head ached because of their conversation and she missed her friend already. At one time in her life, friends surrounded her, but since then she'd killed every last one of them, and now she had no one. When the waiter returned with her daiquiri, she swallowed half of it before it even touched the table. She would've ordered something heavier, but she had to drive.

"I guess I'm meant to be alone," she said to her baby. "It's just me and you against the world."

The moment those words of truth exited her mouth,

her phone rang but the number was blocked which pissed her off. Although she had only given her number to Bricks, Ming and Penny, she couldn't be sure who was calling because Swoopes also had it.

"Hello."

"Yvonna, are you busy?" The woman sounded as if she'd been crying and she was whispering.

"Who is this?"

"Listen, you don't know me, but you should leave Ketchup right away. I can't say anything more."

"What? What are you talkin' about?" *Click!* "Hello! Hello! Who is this?" *Silence.*

Yvonna looked around at all the patrons in her area. No one seemed to be paying her any mind but she was scared shitless. She summoned the waiter over to the table to bring her the check.

"Look, we have to go," she said to him, wiping Delilah's mouth. "I need the check please."

"No problem, mam, would you like a..."

Even if you saw it with your own eyes, you still couldn't believe the sight. The window glass shattered, and the waiter's head was blown completely off his shoulders. Yvonna covered her baby with her body, and hoisted her out of the high chair. It was obvious that the gunman was after her.

"Move!" She screamed running in the back toward the kitchen with her baby tightly in her arms. Delilah was kicking and screaming but Yvonna had her in a death grip and there was no way she was letting her go. "Somebody call the fuckin' police!"

More bullets rang as Yvonna dipped into the swinging door leading to the kitchen, knocking a waiter with a silver tray onto the floor. Bullets continued to bend the stainless steel cabinets, as the gunman gave chase.

"Please stop! I have my little girl in my arms!" She continued to run until she reached a walk in freezer door. A few feet from the freezer, was the back door. She quickly opened the back door and slammed it shut, before she dipped into the freezer. She wanted him to think that she'd gone outside and she hoped it worked. A light switch sat next to the door in the freezer and she cut it off. Her heart beat rapidly as she covered her baby's mouth with her hand.

Peeking through a corner of the freezer door's window, she saw a man she recognized. It was Cane. He walked slowly toward the outside door but not out of it.

"Please go." She sobbed softly. "Please don't hurt my baby."

He remained inside and she hoped he didn't pull on the freezer's door handle because if he had, she would be caught. Although she had her daughter's mouth, she didn't have control of her foot and the baby kicked the door. It sounded off and Yvonna moved quickly away from it. It was too late, he'd heard the noise.

Instead of going outside, he looked at the freezer and smiled. "You in there, bitch?"

It was over. She said a silent prayer for Delilah asking God to let her into heaven, and told the devil she was on her way. Because there was no way they were going to make it out of there alive. The handle continued to move but stopped after loud police sirens sounded in the background. The cops were there and the gunman dashed out the back door.

When she felt he was long gone, she darted out of the freezer and then the restaurant's front door, with her baby in her arms. Out of all of the times she had run for her life, she'd never been as scared as she was at that moment. It wasn't her own life she was concerned about, but that of her baby girl.

She decided then to do what needed to be done. For starters, she would stay with Bricks until she was able to get a place of her own. And then she would grind until she saved up enough cash to leave town. Her mission was simple and concise. Her fight was no longer about revenge, it was about survival.

BRICK'S HOUSE

Bricks walked quickly to the front door to open it for Yvonna. He had known she was coming because his cousin, at the end of the block alerted him that she was on her way. When he opened the door, Yvonna stood motionless, with Delilah in her arms.

"You okay?" He asked pulling them inside. Silence. "You gotta speak to me. Did somebody fuck wit' you? Are you hurt?" He continued as he examined their bodies.

Yvonna stood in the middle of the floor and burst into tears. She hadn't cried that hard since she found out that Bilal was dead. All of the people she murdered, all of the people she'd hurt, and she was finally getting what she deserved and it didn't feel good.

"I'm...I'm...scared," she cried placing Delilah down on the floor for fear she would drop her. "I...I...don't know what to do, Bricks. I don't want to be the other person I use to be. I'm trying to be a good person but it's hard."

Bricks took immediate control over the situation like an anchor in a boat. "Listen, sit down. I got you," he said softly. When she didn't sit down he repeated, "Yvonna...sit down." When she did he said, "Let me tell my brother I'ma hit him back. He outta town right now." He picked up the phone that was sitting on the counter and said, "Melvin, a situation came up, man." He paused and said, "Yeah I'm cool. I'll check you later about them peoples. Hit me when you get back in town."

Yvonna sat on the couch and Bricks opened the basement door and yelled, "Tina! Come up here for a sec!" He looked at Yvonna with pity because he'd never seen her that distraught before. And most of all, he was catching feelings for her.

Tina came up stairs and he said, "Look, take my friend's baby downstairs wit' you, so she can play wit' the girls and Tracy."

Yvonna looked at Tina and although she had a kind face she was nervous about Delilah leaving her sight. "Naw, my baby stays up here wit' me." She said wiping her tears. "I need to make sure she's okay."

"Yvonna," he said calmly, "I ain't gonna let nothin' happen to your baby. You safe, shawty. She's safe. I'll murder somebody if they try to hurt you." He said placing his hand on his chest. "I got it."

Yvonna still sniffling and suffering from a severe headache said, "Okay, but leave the door open. Please."

"We all family here. Relax."

"Like I said," Yvonna repeated, "leave the door open. I gotta hear my baby call if she needs me." Tina saw how torn up Yvonna was and took the child away with no problems and left the door open as she requested.

"So what happened?" Bricks asked after making her a drink of vodka and cranberry juice. "You look like you been through hell."

"Cane tried to kill me at the Harbor! He didn't even

care that I had my baby in my arms. He was fuckin' shootin' and all I could think about was getting' her home safe." She was sobbing all over again and Bricks rubbed her back gently. His strength made her weaker and that scared her. "I done did so many people wrong that the shit has come back to haunt me. But I can't let nobody take her from me. She's all I got."

"You knew this shit was gonna happen. Swoopes' not gonna rest 'til you dead. But think of it this way, in three weeks, we gonna have him right where we want him. We ain't gotta try and find out where he's goin' be, we'll *know* where he's goin' be." Yvonna was listening but made plans to kill Cane early in the AM.

"There ain't gonna be a place on earth that nigga can hide." Bricks continued. "This will all be over soon. Let me grab me somethin' to drink," he said going to the refrigerator to get a beer, the scent of his cologne keeping her company in his absence. While he was gone she used that brief time to check her elbow. And just like he'd said before, she had two moles on it.

"What?" Yvonna asked when he returned with his drink.

"You didn't believe me?" He smirked.

"Believe what?"

"That you had two moles on your elbow," he smiled.

"I wasn't even checking that," she sniffled.

"Yes you were," he said softly. "But you gotta start trustin' me. Just like you checked the moles even after I told you they was there, be the same way you doubt me when I say I know what I'm talkin' 'bout when it comes to this dude. You gotta start trustin' me, Squeeze."

"Squeeze?" she laughed.

"Yeah. That's my new name for you because you stay puttin' me in one."

She smiled liking the corny nickname he'd given her. "We need to hang out. My man's throwin' an all black affair tonight so let's roll through that spot."

"Naw," she said shaking her head. "I'm not in the mood to be going out right now. My best friend's mad at me and me and my baby almost got killed. I just wanna go to sleep and get some rest. You mind if we stay here?"

"I wouldn't want you stayin' any place else." He said putting his arm around the back of her chair. Bricks looked over at her and said, "I don't know why I fuck wit' you but I do. And I know we got off to a bad start but a lot of shit has been goin' on around here and I need a break and I know you need one too. So for me, let me take you out tonight and show you a good time?"

Yvonna's stomach fluttered as she felt his desire to be with her.   "But...but, what about Delilah?"

"Listen, my cousin is the best when it comes to kids. Not only does she have one of her own, she loves bein' around 'em. That's why whenever anybody in the family needs to go somewhere and they got kids, they call her. Your baby couldn't be in better hands. Not to mention, ain't nobody comin' on this block without gettin' blasted. You saw how they held you up down the street. We got niggas on detail outside 24/7 and ain't nobody seen no sign of dude since he left." He placed his hand on her leg and she smiled. "*And*...my cousin a sharp shooter. We had a job to do for my man Kelsi in New York a while back and she handled that shit pregnant." He reminisced. "So trust me, everything cool."

Trust. She thought.

Trust. She thought again.

She had lost so much faith in the word, that it was tough just thinking about it. But she knew if she was going to get to know Bricks, she was going to have to try it, because he was big on it. And after examining the facts, she could tell he had people who would die before they saw any harm come to him. She couldn't have picked a better man to go to war with.

"Okay," she smiled.

"That's what's up." He said excitedly.

They spent the next hour getting ready. Bricks turned on his stereo system, and filled the air with one of Lil Wayne's mix CD's to get them in the mood to go out and have a nice time. She got dressed in Kendal's room, which was odd since she hated her guts, and he got dressed downstairs. She felt giddy thinking that in a moment, she'd be seeing him out of his street clothes and into something grown and sexy.

Yvonna's dress game needed work, and she filled out a little over the years, so she was having a little trouble finding something to wear. But after a while, she settled on a black fitted dress with her three quarter inch boots. Her hips were wider but her stomach was still flat and the weight looked good on her. When she was done, she sat on Kendal's bed and looked around. The closets were empty and the wooden drawers hung open. Debris was everywhere and the entire room needed to be swept. Curious about the woman who hated her so much, she decided to snoop around.

Although all Kendal's clothes were gone, she opened up the drawer fully and saw a brown silicon breast inside. She took it out and sat on the bed to examine it.

"You have gotta be kidding me," she laughed. "The girl was that flat chested? Too each his own," she shrugged before putting the rubber breast back in the drawer.

Looking at herself in the mirror, she determined that she was perfect. On her way out, she walked into Bricks. Her jaw dropped when she saw how fine he looked. Bricks wore all black everything and she couldn't wait to be on his arm.

Wearing a pair of black slacks and black Gucci shoes with the green and red stripe on the heel, it took her back to the days when Terrell use to get dressed and take her out on the town. His build filled the black button down Gucci shirt out with ease. He'd even shaped up his hair in his bathroom so his cut was fresh.

"Damn!" they said at the same time eyeing one another.

They both laughed at their unison.

"Now that's the Yvonna I know," he said taking her hand and spinning her around. "Squeeze, you gonna have niggas going crazy over you tonight. Don't forget about me when you grow up." He continued examining her small waist and thick ass.

When he said that it was brought to her mind that they didn't have an understanding. Outside of needing to get away because all of the drama in their lives, she didn't know if they were going out together or going out as friends.

"So...what are we doing tonight?" Yvonna asked looking at the floor.

"Goin' out." He asked lifting her chin so that her eyes met his grey ones.

"No...I mean, are we going out together or *as friends*?"

"I mean I'm not gonna cock block." He told her thinking she wanted her space.

"I'm not gonna cock block you either," she said back.

"I guess we goin' out as friends," he said backing up a little. A second earlier he was in her space but now he felt he didn't have the right to be. "So let's just have a good time."

"Cool." Yvonna said disappointedly.

Saying goodbye to her baby she was happy to see Delilah playing happily with Tracey and Tina's daughter. Tracey even gave her a hug, which shocked her. Seeing the smile on Delilah's face, and how good Tina was with children put her mind at ease.

Before leaving, Bricks called his cousins and told them he was pulling out because three of his boy cousins were going too and the rest were watching the block. The family knew that someone was to keep an eye on Bricks at all times. Losing a family member simply wasn't acceptable.

Bricks and Yvonna were almost out the door when they opened it and saw Bet crying on the front step. She was beaten and frantic. "They...they got my baby! They gonna kill my baby, Bricks! Please don't let 'em kill my child!"

Forty yelled, "I called your cell to tell you she was on the way. It was Bet so I let her on the block," he said realizing no one should've gotten that close without notification.

"Go in the house, Yvonna," he said looking around the street. When she didn't leave he pushed her inside, "Get the fuck in the house!" he wasn't sure what was up and didn't want her getting hurt.

Two of his cousins had already run across the street and they lifted Bet off the ground and into the house. Once inside, she desperately tried to catch her breath.

"What happened, Bet?" Bricks asked as they watched her crumple up on the floor.

"I...I left the store, and a car rammed into the side of mine. At first I thought it was an accident so I got out." Bricks shook his head at her first mistake. "Then they...they...put a gun to my head and asked me if I knew you. I said no and they hit me in the face." She sobbed. "When I admitted I did, they handed me this, and told me to tell you it was on. Please, Bricks, don't let 'em kill my Kendal."

Bricks looked at the picture and saw Kendal covered in blood, with her mouth gagged and her arms and ankles tied together. The picture read, '*This could've been avoided. It's your move.*'

THREE'S A FUCKIN' PROBLEM

Bricks and his cousins Forty, Russo and Jace strolled into Topaz Hotel and headed towards the bar. They were going to a private party held by Cameo, a kingpin in Northwest DC, who they dealt business with. Yvonna was shocked when she saw the plush couches tailored in turquoise alligator print. The lounge was cozy, quiet and quaint and she'd never heard of it before. She was expecting a louder rowdier crowd, and got a milder sexier one instead. It was certainly refreshing considering all of the drama she endured earlier that day.

"What up, man?" Cameo said to Bricks embracing him in a manly one-arm hug. "I thought ya'll wasn't comin' through." He clasped each of Bricks cousins too.

"We had drama at the fort, but it ain't nothin' we can't handle."

"You need my help?" Cameo said looking at him as he placed his hands on his chest. Bricks knew he was being extra for Yvonna, but he let him slide.

"Naw, we got it."

"Cool...cool...and who's this?" The way he eyed her without consideration of who she was with made her uneasy.

Everything was perfect on his body from the heels of his imprinted Louis Vuitton black leather shoes, to the tip of his head. He modeled a pair of black slacks, a black designer dress jacket and a black button shirt with a few buttons open at the top for swagger's sake. "I ain't seen you around D.C. before."

"I told you, Squeeze" Bricks said in a low voice to Yvonna. He was referring to their conversation earlier about how he knew the men would be all over her.

"Oh...this you?" Cameo asked hearing the name he'd given her.

"Naw...this just my homie," he said although his eyes said something else. "And, Yvonna, this my man Cameo."

Yvonna shook his hand softly and smiled, "It's nice to meet you."

"Likewise," he said so smoothly, she was shocked. Any other time if a dude would've hit her with the word, 'likewise' she would've thought of him as a gump, but Cameo was different and she liked that. "If you need anything let me know, Squeeze."

"I'm sorry, only Bricks and call me Squeeze. But you can all me Yvonna."

His cousins looked at Bricks and smiled.

"Cool...cool." Cameo said. "I get what's goin' on here." He said looking between Yvonna and Bricks who had pulled her a little closer without even knowing. "Well, your table is over there man, and you know whatever you want on the bar, I got that. We'll talk lata 'bout that gift."

Yvonna was no fool, she knew the *gift* he was referring to was weight and she was more curious about the man who stood before her than ever. Bricks was turning out to be more interesting by the minute.

"You know you ain't have to do that for me." Brick's said with his hand resting gently in the small of her back. "Cameo's pretty good peoples."

"What you talkin' 'bout?" Yvonna pretended as if she didn't know.

"You know, tellin' him not to call you Squeeze."

"I told him not to call me that because he couldn't. Wasn't nobody doin' nothin' for you. You want me keepin' time with other niggas in here for real, Bricks? Just say the word."

"I'm not even goin' to dignify that shit wit' a response."

Bricks cousins went deeper into the den of well-mannered drug dealers while they walked toward the table. Once she sat down, she called Tina's cell phone which she had given her, to check on Delilah. She was fine. Bricks and Yvonna were quiet for five minutes and seemed to be in a zone. There was so much sexual tension between them that it was hard not to notice.

"Why you starin' at me, girl?" Bricks said after he rubbed his hands together coolly and looked at her. Yvonna looked behind him and saw his cousins watching attentively to be sure he was okay.

"You're family loves you don't they?" she asked.

Bricks looked behind him, turned back around and said, "We close. It's always been that way. My grandmother had a big family and all of her kids got caught up on that crack shit. Some dead some locked up and the others just lost. When we got older, we all found each other and kept our bond. It's been that way ever since."

"What's up wit' your fam?" he asked.

"I don't have one," her tone was soft. Not trying to ruin

the mood she said, "This a nice spot."

One of Jay-Z's songs filled the room and she bopped her head to the music trying not to appear nervous. But why was she? She felt like an idiot with a schoolgirl crush all at the same time.

"Yeah, it's cool. Cameo knows how to throw nice joints."

"You know we didn't have to come out right? I mean, after what happened to Bet and wit' Kendal bein' missing. I would've understood if you wanted to stay home."

Bricks looked away as if he was contemplating what he was going to say. But when his eyes met hers again, he was very confident. "Shawty, let me put you down wit' somethin', I don't do shit I don't wanna do. Not to mention niggas been shootin' at us all week. So we not gonna go out 'cause somebody else got hemmed up?" he said shaking his head. "I'm my own man and I make my own decisions. Now, that shit wit' Bet is fucked up. And I'm not gonna lie, I don't like the fact that this dude got her peoples jammed up. But he took enough of my time this week and I can't allow him to take no more. Shit gonna pan out how it's gonna pan out. Besides, I'm tryin' to see what's up wit' other things."

"Things?" she said softly.

"Yeah...things." He said slyly looking at her.

"You look at me differently? Why?"

"What you mean?" he asked sitting back into his chair.

"I remember when we used to hang out, you told me you could never be wit' anybody serious. How come you don't want a girlfriend?"

"You know...I really don't know." He shrugged. "I guess I like makin' money, with relative ease. Sometimes ya'll females can fuck shit up. Look at all the shit that's happening now."

"Bricks if you want me gone I can leave," she said getting up.

"Why you do that shit? Always runnin'? You asked me a question and I answered it. Sit down, Yvonna." He said not even looking at her. She sat down and looked around to see who was watching. "I'm not the type of dude to fall in love," he said looking deeply into her eyes. "But maybe one day all that'll change. Get it?"

"Yeah." She smiled.

"You want somethin' to eat or drink? I'm 'bout to go to the bar."

"Oh...yeah, a Ciroc martini."

Bricks got up to get the drinks and she went with him with her eyes. She saw all of the women looking at him and eventually one slithered up next to him and she frowned. What really fucked her up was when he faced the girl, wrapped his arm around her waist, and kissed her passionately in the mouth. Yvonna was flushed with embarrassment as everyone started pointing and laughing at her. She felt humiliated that she came in there with him only for him to embarrass her.

She stormed up to him and said, "Why you disrespectin' me?!"

"What?" he said staring at her with piercing eyes.

"You just kissed that girl in front of me and I came here wit' you! If you wanna carry it like that you can just take me home!"

"Yvonna, I ain't kiss nobody. What the fuck is you talkin' 'bout?"

She looked around and everybody she thought was staring at her, was doing regular shit. And the woman she thought she'd seen kissing him was suddenly not even there. Once again, the doctor's voice entered her mind.

But always...always...take your medicine. If you don't your mind will convince you of the most absurd things and you'll find yourself in the craziest of situations.'

"Are you okay?" He asked sincerely placing his hand on her shoulder.

"Uh...yeah. It must've been somebody else. I'ma go sit down."

Yvonna took her seat and waited for him to return with the drinks hoping he wouldn't bring up the matter again.

"Look, I'ma make a few rounds, you gonna be cool?" Bricks said dropping the drinks off to table.

"Yeah...uh...I'll be fine," She said not wanting to really be alone.

"I'm not gettin' with no other chicks or nothin'," he joked. "Just gonna handle business."

Great. Now I look like a basket case. She had to redeem herself. "Bricks you can do whatever you want to do, 'cause I am too."

The smile was removed off of his face and he said, "Well have fun."

"I will." She said without looking at him.

He was turning around to leave until he said, "And don't worry 'bout Swoopes coming through here," he assured her with his eyes. "It's so much money in this room, you gotta be the President to get through them doors."

She wanted to relax but it was easier said than done. After all, she had just freaked out. She'd never had an instance like that happen during her illness. Seeing people was one thing seeing situations was another. She decided she didn't want to be alone.

"Would it be okay if I invited Ming?"

"That Chinese chick?"

"Yeah."

"That's your home girl ain't it?' he smiled.

"Yeah, she's my peoples."

"Well I'll tell Cameo to expect her. So call her up and tell her it's cool. You got my cell so call me if you need me."

Yvonna called Ming who hung up the first three times, but after a while, she was able to get her to listen with the words, "I'll do it."

Thirty minutes later, Ming strolled into the lounge with Darcus on her arm. They looked cute together and complimented each other very well. The moment Ming hit the floor, in her black one-piece mini dress, all mouths dropped. She was stuntin' on them bitches with her full-length black Christian Louboutin boots and black waist leather jacket. And when she saw the black leather Mia Bossi bag, an expensive high-end diaper bag, she knew she'd probably just dropped off Boy. But Yvonna was frustrated seeing Darcus because she wanted this to be their time alone. They had a lot to discuss and he would be in the way.

"Where's the baby?" Yvonna asked as Ming and Darcus sat across from her at the table.

"My aunt has him. Ming picks him up when she leaves in the morning."

Yvonna decided to excuse Darcus who had obviously decided he wasn't going to follow the dress code, from the table. He still looked sexy in his jeans and black leather jacket, so she would let it pass.

"Darcus, can you give me and her a moment?"

"Not a problem," he smiled before getting up. "You can have all the time ya need."

"Ming, what's up?" Yvonna asked getting right to the point.

"I am niece of Yao Chen, drug lord of the Mah Jong

Dynasty, and we are Legion."

"Okay now you scarin' me. Last time I heard that Legion word I was watching the movie 'The Exorcist'."

A tear fell down Ming's face and she wiped it away. "Ming is serious and she needs you to listen. Legion in your culture means thousands."

"I'm sorry...I was just playin'...go 'head."

"Like I said, my uncle is the lord of the Mah Jong Dynasty. In disguise it is social club in China. Mah Jong is a game played by four players, which involves skill, strategy and calculation. Same traits needed to be good in drug game. In China, my family does well with drug business, but now, uncle wants territory here in America. I knew this day would come because uncle brought my family over here and opened a nail salon in my name for us to work in. At first we were happy because we all together, and then, he started bringing over people not from family.

"Just last month, my uncle open ten more nail salons, for which I am owner. They all fronts for cocaine trade. And he's sending over more people from China to help, many of which I don't like. But they are skilled in Wushu and weaponry, just as I am."

"Fuck is a Wushu?"

"A form of martial arts."

"You can fight?" Yvonna laughed.

"I can kill." She wasn't laughing anymore. "We also good with most weapons used by people in your streets and your military. But trust me Yvonna, the training is the most painful thing I'd ever endured. Ming wouldn't wish it on worse enemy."

Yvonna was stunned. She figured Ming moved a few bricks from time to time after seeing the duffle bag at Ketchup, but this was ridiculous. "So how does the cocaine and New York thing tie in together?"

"My uncle has had problems breaking in on the trade here in D.C. and Maryland, but has been successful in New York. He has accepted much money from a dealer there and now we must deliver."

"So what's the problem? Aren't you going to China for business? Since your uncle wants you in New York, can't he just give you a pass and let you go to China the next day?"

"I go to China to make good with mother," she said putting her hand on her chest. Tears flooded her eyes and ran down her face. She was emotionally broken down again. "When...when I first came here, to America for uncle Yao, mother not happy about it. She knew he was using me. She has been fighting with her brother for two decades over his selfishness and cruelty. I thought mother was just angry that with uncle Yao I had a chance to leave China and make good for myself. In China my uncle is a big deal. So against my mother's will, I left and she made it known throughout our family that I was dead to her.

"At first I didn't care because I had money, cars and power. But then, I got to see man my uncle Yao really is. So I would go to China for months and beg at my mother's feet, each time she would walk away after hearing my pleas. She won't even acknowledge her grandson, Boy. I had him, thinking she would learn to love me again. It didn't work." She paused. "But last trip, she has finally agreed to hear me out and offers me one day to make it right. And that day is tomorrow. If I don't go I'll lose my mother for good. And I need my mother."

Although Yvonna didn't know what it was like to have a mother's love, she certainly understood what it was like to be without it. "Can't you just tell your uncle you wanna make up wit' your mother? Is he that fucked up to deny you?"

"He is evil man. I told him and he laughed in my face earlier today before I met you at restaurant. I was so angry that I slapped him in the face. He got mad, and grabbed my hair, and spit in my mouth. He likes drama. It does him good to know my mother...his sister...might cut me off forever. He plays me against her to forsake her. But if you make the drop, with Darcus, two people Ming trusts, then Ming can serve tea to her mother."

"Serve tea? Shouldn't you be buying her ass a fly Gucci bag or somethin'?"

"In China, it is tradition to serve tea when one is in submission and sorry. As I am."

Yvonna exhaled after hearing an earful. She felt like she went to China and back. "Do you think your uncle would try to kill me?"

"My uncle would kill anybody to get his way." Yvonna's stomach churned. "But it is unlikely that he tried to kill you, because he knows little of you. Why?"

"A long story." She was referring to the bullet spree at the restaurant.

Ming reached over and grabbed her hand. "Will you help me?"

"Who you gonna tell your uncle made the drop?"

"He has worked with Darcus before, and things were good. I'll tell him the both of you are going for me, *after* I'm on plane."

"Okay.

"Thank you so much! Ming loves you for this."

"Ming needs to pay me for this too." Yvonna said sarcastically. "I'm takin' a big risk."

"How much you ask?"

"Since your feelings are hurt I'm not gonna hit you too hard," they both laughed, "although I know you are sittin' on millions."

"Ming knew you would snoop around eventually, so Ming left bank statement lying around. It was Ming's way of telling you a little of her life at a time."

"Cool, I just need a little to get back on top and to set me and Delilah up. So, let's say fifty thousand?"

"You got it."

Yvonna felt a weight lifted off of her shoulders and then she looked at Darcus. He was still staring at her and she wasn't sure if he was a rapist or what. Whatever issues he had, she knew he had better get over them. If he knew what was good for him.

BAD BLOOD

"I can't believe you still talkin' 'bout this," Yvonna said entering Brick's house. She threw her purse on the sofa and placed her hands on her hips ready to get into his shit. "How was I to know Darcus and Cameo had beef?

"You wouldn't," he said closing the door, tossing his keys on the counter, "But I told you, you could invite the Chinese chick, not anotha nigga."

"Do you want me to call Cameo and apologize? 'Cause all this you doin' ain't even necessary. It was a mistake on my part. I didn't even expect Ming to bring his ass wit' her. When I looked up, he was just there. Whateva' happened to that shit about only the President bein' able to get through the doors? Huh?"

"Why do you breed so much drama?" He said to himself.

"So you really blamin' me for everything, includin' Ming bringin' Darcus?"

"You know what...this arrangement might not work after all. Maybe you should stay over your home girl's house or somethin'. My brother was right about you. You got too much shit wit' you."

She was hurt that his brother, a man she'd never met, had already forged an opinion of her. "And you wonder why I run." She said looking at him. "This why."

"I'm not tryin' to even hear all of this shit right now."

"So you puttin' me out?" she paused. She could've gone over Ming's but suddenly, she didn't want to. "Whateva happened to you bein' there for me? You forgot about that already?"

"Hey, Bricks," Tina said entering the living room from the basement, "Delilah is sleep downstairs." She put her jacket on and dangled her car keys, "I had my sister bring over my baby's old portable playpen and some toys, so Delilah's good," she said to Yvonna. "She layin' on it fast asleep."

"Thank you." Yvonna sighed. "I really appreciate it."

"No problem."

"Where your kids?" He asked.

"Greek came and got my kids and Tracey earlier today. You know their father can't be wit'out 'em too long."

He smiled and said, "Thanks for everything today, cuzo."

"You know we family. But is everything okay, here?" She asked looking at him. There was concern in her voice and Yvonna could tell that if Bricks said the wrong thing, she and his cousin would be engaged in a full fledge fist-fight.

"Uh...yeah, everything cool."

"Aight...Melvin called and said he back in town. He'll be over tomorrow."

"Cool." He said looking at Yvonna, who was walking around gathering her shit. His eyes said he wanted her to stop so that they could finish their conversation. But he had to wait to be away from his cousin's watchful eyes. "Let me walk you outside."

"And I'ma go get my baby," Yvonna said.

"Don't wake her up yet."

"You said you want me gone, so I'm gone."

"Just wait...please." He said holding the door for his cousin.

"Five minutes." She said.

Bricks walked Tina outside and came back inside. "Sit down."

"I gotta get ready to leave. You put me out remember?" She continued walking towards the bedroom to change her clothes.

"Yvonna, sit the fuck down!"

She stopped in her tracks but she didn't sit down. "Make up your mind, Bricks. Do you want me to leave or stay? You can't have it both ways."

"I don't fuckin' know right now. I'm not use to this shit!" He said to himself. "I know I shouldn't be fuckin' wit' you." He pointed at her. "And I know you shouldn't be in my crib, but I gotta make sure you aight."

"That's the only thing you wanna do? Make sure I'm aight? 'Cause if that's the case, I can call you everyday."

"See how you still runnin' your mouth? Now I know you use to talkin' to dudes any kinda way but that ain't gonna work wit' me. Now sit down!"

"What's up wit' you and this sittin' down shit?"

"Please." He said pointing to the couch.

When she was seated he said, "That Jamaican cat your home girl fuckin' wit' ain't good peoples."

"Why?"

"I'm tellin' you too much but since we in a lot of shit together already I'ma put this on your plate too. He use to be our weed connect, but he got greedy and started overchargin' niggas. The last time we dealt wit' him, it was on a package he shorted us on. A lot of bodies dropped over somethin' that coulda been handled man to man. Cameo got the short end of that transaction. We ain't see each other again 'til tonight." Bricks flicked his shoes off. "Matta fact, I don't even know why he's here. He lives in Jamaica or some shit. How your girl know his ass anyway?"

"I don't know how she knows him," she said, leaving out how just the other day she had his dick in her mouth while Ming ate her pussy. "It was my first time meetin' him tonight."

"Well you better tell your girl to stay the fuck away from him."

"What Ming does with her pussy is her choice. I can't make her stop seein' nobody she don't want to."

"And you call yourself a friend?" He laughed. "Wit' friends like you, who need enemies?"

"You finished?" she asked looking over at him. "Since you like women to say as little as possible I certainly don't wanna interrupt you."

"I'm done."

"So I guess I'll be gettin' my baby and my stuff to leave."

"I don't want you to leave. Not tonight anyway. If you wanna go tomorrow, that's cool wit' me, you can do what you want. But you shouldn't be taken that baby out this house tonight."

She knew Delilah wasn't the only person he was concerned about. Brick's eyes told her she held a place in his heart.

"Well I guess I'ma go to sleep." Before she walked downstairs she said, "Do you think your cousin Tina can watch Delilah for me tomorrow? I got somethin' to do early."

"Maybe." He said looking at her. "She got some things goin' on during the day, but she may be able to handle it. I'll call her tonight."

"Oh, can I stay downstairs instead of bringing the baby up here?" she said walking to the door. She really wasn't ready to go to bed but she couldn't just tell him. She wanted to be around him but her stubbornness wouldn't allow her to. "I don't feel comfortable sleepin' in Kendal's room."

"Yeah. I'll pull the sofa bed out for you." He said staring into her eyes.

"What?" She asked.

"Nothin'," he spat back.

Bricks got the bed together and Yvonna washed up and jumped into it. Delilah was fast asleep in the portable playpen, which was also a bed, a few feet away from her. She liked having Delilah around.

In bed alone, she thought about what Bricks said. Who needs enemies when you have friends like you? She made up her mind to tell Ming about Darcus.

When she grabbed her phone out of her purse, she realized it was off. She turned if off by accident earlier that day and forgot. The moment the screen lit up, she saw twenty voicemails and they were all from Penny. She listened to a couple of them and erased most. But one voicemail she heard caused her to sit up straight in the bed.

"Yvonna, yous got a hour to bring my baby home or I'm callin' the police!"

"What the fuck?" she said looking at the handset. "This bitch has lost her fuckin' mind."

She knew she would trip when it was time for her to

take her baby but she didn't realize how attached she'd gotten. She decided not to feed into Penny's bullshit for the minute and as long as she didn't try to take her child away, she'd be fine.

She redirected her attention to Ming and called her. "Ming, it's Yvonna. You up?"

"Yes. Ming has big day tomorrow. What's up?" She said in a sleepy voice.

"You left before a lot of shit broke out. But apparently, Darcus has bad blood with Bricks and Cameo. They say he shorted them on a package and everything. Maybe you shouldn't have him goin' wit' me to New York."

She yawned and said, "Ming knows, he told me about it when we left."

"What did he say?"

"Ming, can't remember everything, Yvonna. Just that they use to deal with each other and now they don't. No need to worry, he's fine. That was many years ago."

"Ming does that man have your nose *and* your pussy wide open?"

"If Ming isn't worried, you shouldn't be either."

"Bricks told me to tell you to stay away from him."

She laughed and said, "Ming's a big girl."

"Where is he?" Yvonna asked frustrated. She didn't want to see her only friend get in over her head, especially after being introduced to her issues with her uncle Yao.

"He's right here... watching TV."

Yvonna couldn't believe Darcus was next to her while she was on the phone, when he was the topic of their discussion. "Ming, you trippin' so I'ma let you go in a minute but I hope for your sake you know what you doing. When am I pickin' up the package?"

"Day after tomorrow, at my house. Darcus will be here waiting on you."

"Wait, you gonna to leave the bags wit' him?"

"Yes. He'll have everything you need to know when you get here."

"But shouldn't I examine them wit' you? What if somethin' happens?"

"It won't," Ming said nonchalantly. "I trust him."

It was then that Yvonna made up her mind that Ming couldn't make sound decisions. So, she would have to rid the world of Darcus herself.

"What time you want me there?"

"Early."

"Cool. But does your cousin still own that 24 hour carry out spot?"

"Yeah why?" Ming yawned again.

"Look, I'ma need you tomorrow before you leave."

"Ming has to be on plane!"

"It'll be real quick? Can you get a uniform from your cousin and her delivery car and drive it to an address I'ma give you? Oh...and I'ma also need a hose and some antifreeze."

"Yvonna! That's too much for Ming to do tomorrow!"

"It sounds like a lot but it's not. Your part will take all of five minutes." Ming sighed. When she felt Ming's hesitation she decided to hammer home. "Look, I ain't wanna get into a lot of shit wit' you today but somebody tried to kill me and my baby earlier. Now I'm not gonna be able to get at Swoopes, but I can do some other things to one of his men. So will you help me or not?"

"How early?"

"Six in the morning. I figure you can have your cousin bring you the carry out car and the uniform tonight. Let her drive one of your other cars home."

"Okay...I'll do it," Ming relented. "Give me the information."

Yvonna spent the next ten minutes going over her plan, and she felt it was almost perfect. A few minutes later, Bricks came downstairs.

"You sleep?" he asked standing on the steps. The light from the hallway lit up his muscular silhouette and Yvonna could smell the soap from his body. In her opinion, there was nothing like a clean man.

"Not really...why?" She said adjusting the sheets on the bed.

"You want some company?"

She could've said no but she didn't want to be alone. "I don't care."

Bricks walked down the stairs and eased into bed with her. She turned to her side and he wrapped his arms around her waist pulling her to him. She melted into him. "You awfully forward." Yvonna said. "How you know I want you touchin' me?"

"Cause you turned that ass my way."

Yvonna playfully hit him. "I always sleep on my side."

"Stop playin', girl, after all that fussin' upstairs. You know you want me in this bed," he continued as he pulled her closer. "Just like I wanna be in this bed wit' you."

It felt good.

It felt right.

"We can't fuck so don't try nothing," she said turning her head to look at him after feeling the bulge in his shorts on her ass. "My baby's in this room."

"Still ain't trynna give up the pussy."

"I'm serious."

"You real overprotective of her ain't you?"

"I guess so." She said turning her head back around, focusing on the playpen. "She's all I got."

"I get that." He said rubbing her shoulder.

"Bricks," she paused sinking into his touch. She wasn't sure if she wanted to say the next thing, but if she didn't, she wouldn't know if they had a real chance to be. "Kendal was right." She said softly. "About what she said."

Silence.

"Did you hear me?" she asked turning her head toward him again.

"Yeah." He said hesitantly.

"I suffer from schizophrenia. Apparently all my life."

Silence.

"What does that mean? I ain't neva heard of nobody in real life havin' no shit like that before."

Yvonna sighed and said, "I don't fully understand it either. I do know I can control it a little more than I use to. But basically it means that sometimes I see people and things that aren't really there."

"Like today in the club?"

She was so embarrassed she wanted to hide under Penny's ass. "Yes. If I take my medication, like I been doin', I'll be fine. But sometimes...I... I feel I need my illness, to make me stronger."

Bricks didn't know what to say to her crazy ass. Although he had to admit, he'd never met anybody like her.

"Why you say that?"

"When I don't take my medicine, I see someone named Gabriella. In the earlier stages of my condition, she could take over my body all together. Now, as long as I take my medicine, it doesn't happen that much. If I take the full dose, I'm drowsy and don't feel right but if I take a half a pill, my hallucinations slow down. But if I miss one day or more, my illness can take over and people can get hurt."

"Who told you all this shit? Them white people?" he

said looking at her. "You know damn well don't no black people have no skitz-a-whateva the fuck you just said. Only white people get that kinda shit. Ain't nothin' wrong wit' you, girl. You just be trippin' sometimes that's all."

"I'm serious, Bricks. I mean...I know we only gonna be together for the next three weeks, until this shit blows over, but I just wanted to tell you. You know, wit' you lettin' me stay here and all."

"You not gonna kill me or nothin' are you?" He asked half seriously.

"Naw...I'ma let you live," she said pushing her ass into him deeper.

"Listen, 'bout tomorrow, I'm askin' you not to do anything alone." He said remembering something she'd said earlier. "If you wanna hit up whoever, I'ma do it wit' you. Just don't leave without lettin' me know."

"This my drama not yours. I just wanna kick up some shit like Swoopes did to me that's all."

"If you think I'm lettin' you handle this shit by yourself you don't know me. Now what time we gettin' up?"

"I'ma get up at 11:00 in the morning." She lied.

"Just wake me up wit' you. I'm not an early bird."

"Okay," she said closing her eyes.

But when the morning came, and Bricks reached out for her, she was already gone.

LUBE JOB

"Carry out! Open the door please."

Cane jumped out of bed, rubbed his eyes and listened to what he thought were quick raps at his front door. When two louder bangs followed, he hopped out of bed and moved toward the sound. Once he made it to the front door, he looked outside and saw a small Chinese man with a blue cap on his head and a brown paper bag in his hands. At the curb sat a Ford Mercury with a 'We Come 24/7', sign on top of it.

"Who the fuck knockin' at my door at 6:00 in the mornin'?!" Cane yelled rubbing his hand on his bare chest.

"We Come 24-7!" Someone said in a thick Chinese accent. Cane rubbed his eyes and looked through the peephole. "You pay now or we leave."

"I ain't order no fuckin' food!"

"Look...we come 'cause you place order! Either you pay now, or we band address off list! Your choice...we don't care."

Cane was about to curse him out and send him on his way, when his stomach growled. Although he didn't order the food, he was hungry. "What's in the order?"

The Chinese man opened the brown paper bag and examined the contents. When he finished he said, "Pancakes, sausage and eggs. Do you want or not?"

Sleepy and not thinking straight, he opened the door and was met with a severe blow to the face by a bat. Yvonna, who was standing on the side of his house out of view, rushed inside.

"What the fuck is this?" He asked, angry he left his gun in the back room.

"Payback, bitch!" She yelled hitting him in the head again with the bat, rendering him unconscious.

Twenty minutes later, when Cane came to, he was strapped to a leather chair, with his arms and legs bound.

"Look, Ming has to go! Hurry up and tie!" Ming said as she helped Yvonna finish up the last few knots. They were talking around Cane as if he were an article of clothing and a not a real person.

"Bitch, I'm moving as fast as I can," Yvonna said tying the last knot.

When they were done, Ming stood up and removed the cap she used to disguise herself as a man. Her bob cut hairstyle flopped out and she ran her fingers through her hair.

"Okay, we're done. Ming must go. Next time we kill at a more convenient time." Yvonna smiled. "And don't forget about the trip tomorrow," she continued before leaving out the door.

When Ming was gone, Yvonna sat in the chair across from Cane. She looked sexy in her jean skirt, and corset shaped black leather jacket. So she could maneuver around comfortably, instead of wearing high heel boots, she opted for her black comfortable Uggs.

"Cane is it?" Yvonna said flicking a match and lighting a cigarette. "Do you remember me?"

"Of course he does," Gabriella said. "Kill his ass."

Although her illness had gotten more manageable, as far as she was concerned, it was still difficult to hear her voice and not have a negative reaction to it.

"For real, I started not to come back here," he said slowly, "'Cause I knew you had my address. But I was sure you ain't see my face at the restaurant. I guess I was wrong."

She smiled. "Since you know so much, what am I gonna do now?"

"I was hopin' you'd wanna make some cash, to put this all behind us."

Although she hadn't planned on robbing Cane, now that the offer was on the table, it didn't sound half bad. "Where's the money and how much we talkin'?"

"It's not here. I can get it though. We can go together."

Yvonna spoke through stiff lips and said, "You think I'm a fuckin' fool?"

"No...but you look like a smart woman. And I figured you'd recognize a good opportunity if it fell in your lap." Cane appealed.

"So what's the price of my baby's life? Since that's what we talkin' about right? You want me to forget that you almost killed my baby and me yesterday. So to you, how much is that worth?"

"Kill him, Yvonna," Gabriella said walking behind her to speak in her ear. "You didn't stop taking your medicine to just hear me talk...unleash me."

Yvonna stood up, and walked over to him. "Open your mouth."

"What?" The moment he spoke, she put the cigarette out on his lips and his jaws flew open. When it did, she shoved a black tube to the back of his throat. When he bit down on it, she punched him again reopening his mouth.

"Keep your fuckin' mouth open. Do you hear me?" Yvonna said standing over him. He nodded in agreement. "Good. Now...I'm gonna ask you a couple of questions," She said removing a pair of brown leather gloves from her back pocket. "And you gonna give me the answers. Do you understand me so far?" Again he nodded. "Good. Where does Swoopes live?"

He didn't respond and she punched him in the stomach. "Where?" She repeated, but again he remained silent. This time she took a large bottle of antifreeze, removed the top and connected the spout to a white plastic pump that connected to the hose inside his mouth. She made the little concoction in Brick's garage before she went to Cane's house.

"This is too good!" Gabriella said. "I could not have thought of a better way to torture him myself."

"I'm sure you could have," Yvonna laughed.

"W...what's this...for?" he mumbled despite the tube being lodged down his throat.

"You don't want to answer my questions, so we'll play another game."

Yvonna hit the pump twice and two large swallows of antifreeze entered the tube and rolled down his throat. The sweetness was unexpected and seemed less frightening until he felt his stomach rumble.

"Where...does...Swoopes live?" She repeated. "I know you didn't mean to hurt me and my baby." She said in a sweet soft tone. "But I also know he sent you. So let him endure all of this instead of you. It's only fair. So tell me...where is he?"

He was determined to remain silent, so she pumped the nozzle three more times and more liquid oozed down his throat. When it did, he felt a whirlwind in his stomach as vomit reached his throat and escaped his mouth, splashing everywhere. Yvonna jumped back just in time to prevent his bodily fluids from soaking her shoes.

"Now...where does he live?" She asked trying not to inhale the terrible smell.

"P...please. Don't do this shit." He mumbled as his body moved in violent convulsions. "You...you ain't gotta do this."

Yvonna's eyebrows creased and she pumped twice more. "No! You ain't gotta do this! All you have to do is tell me where the fuck he lives! Don't be stupid. I will kill you in here today."

Instead of answering he just closed his eyes. He knew it was over and it appeared he was ready to meet his fate.

"Do it again," Gabriella cheered. "He still doesn't get the picture so you gotta make him feel it." Yvonna pumped the antifreeze into his body again. "Once more!"

She continued to strike the pump until Cane regurgitated so much, that the fluid leaving his body turned to blood and his eyes drooped. Angry couldn't explain how Yvonna felt because she found someone loyal to the one man she felt deserved to rot in hell.

"You sure you don't wanna tell me where he lives?"

Inaudible words left his mouth and Yvonna moved closer to hear him better.

"F... y... b..." He said.

"What?"

The moment she got closer, he threw up all over her clothes. He had held his own vomit, in his mouth, just to throw up on her when she got closer. Blood, food particles and mucus covered her leather jacket, ran down her legs and hit her soft boots.

"I said, fuck you bitch!" He said as audible as possible.

"Your funeral!" She yelled striking him so hard in the face, his nose broke under her fist. With his mouth still open, she poured the liquid down his throat. Fluid eased out the sides and fell onto the floor. He could no longer breathe or fight. And when his body stopped moving, she allowed the plastic bottle to fall at her feet. This was not the ending she'd hoped for.

"Fuck him," Gabriella said. "You gonna have to smoke Swoopes out yourself."

"I know...but this shit gonna definitely piss him off."

"I hope you ready."

"I was born that way."

BABY MAMA DRAMA

After leaving Target to buy a new pair of jeans and shirt, since Cane ruined her others, she went to the library to do some research. It only took her a couple of hours and a few phone calls to find out what she needed to know to exact her next plan.

After the library she visited Mom's and purchased a couple of Speed pills. And later she arranged to meet with a local manufacturer of Lidocaine, a powdered substance generally used to make gels to prevent itching. But she had two hours before he could be ready and he was closing briskly afterwards. He wasn't supposed to be even selling her the powder, but she offered him enough money to make it worth his while. She was just about to get on 295, leading to Virginia when Bricks called.

"Yes Bricks?" She hesitated knowing Bricks would be angry that she left without waking him up.

"Shawty, I know you ain't do what I asked you not to."

"I had to." She sighed maneuvering down the busy

road in early morning traffic. She tossed a few new CD cases around that she'd bought at Target before settling on Mariah Carey's, *An Imperfect Angel*, CD.

"You had to?" He repeated. "You okay?"

"I'm talkin' ain't I?"

Bricks sighed and said, "And you left your kid here without any milk. What kinda shit is that?"

"So you can babysit Chomps but not my daughter?" She paused only to breathe. "And don't you have some milk left from the cereal Tracey ate? And what happened to your cousin watching her for me?"

"What?! Yo...I feel like mashin' on your ass right now."

"Bricks, what you want me to do?"

"Come get your fuckin' kid."

"I can't right now. I have something I have to do right quick."

"You bringing that dude to the spot last night caused me to have to meet up wit' Cameo. And to be honest," he said growing angrier. "It don't matter what my fuckin' reason is. You don't do no unmotherly shit like leave your kid wit' somebody without checkin' to make sure everything is cool."

"Unmotherly shit?!" She yelled. "You got me fucked –"

She was so mad about what he said, that she slammed into the back of a car at the light. When the driver got out, the rage in his face frightened her.

"If this nigga's smart, he'll get back in the fuckin' car," Gabriella said filing her nails.

"Bricks, hold on, I just got into an accident."

Yvonna stepped out of the car and got closer to the angry driver. She was pissed when she saw that the only damage he had was a knick to his black paint. It was so small you could barely see it.

"What the fuck is wrong with you?!" he screamed

pointing to his black BMW. "ARE YOU ASLEEP OR FUCKIN' DRIVIN'!?"

"Look...ain't shit wrong wit' your car," she said turning around to walk away. "So stop bein' a fuckin' sissy."

She gave him her ass to kiss and strutted back to her car. But the moment she opened the car door to slide into her seat, he placed his banana hand on the handle, preventing her from closing it fully. Now he had fucked up.

"You got five seconds to get the fuck off my car." She said calmly.

"Bitch, you betta get back out here and wait for the police," he said maintaining his hold on her door. "Think you gonna hit a nigga's car and roll out?"

Yvonna positioned her body so that her feet were sitting flatly on the street, and then she looked around only to see mounds of people watching.

"I can't stand rubberneckers!" she said out loud.

She hated them even more considering they were also witnesses. Thinking on her feet, she hung up on Bricks, and went to the video camera setting on her phone. When she was there, she held it in her hands. But she didn't record just yet.

The moment he turned away, she took her long foot and kicked his phone out of his hands. It fell to the ground and crashed into a bunch of tiny pieces. Now it was time for action so she hit the record button on the phone and positioned it in her lap.

Pissed she'd just broken his phone, he lunged toward her in full attack mode. And this sudden act of violence is what the witnesses saw. She allowed him to approach her and put his hands on her throat. But when she had enough, she kicked him in his penis and he doubled over and fell to the ground.

Then she screamed, "Rape!" and kicked him in his mouth while he was down. "Somebody help me!"

Sure it was mighty convenient that the man whose car she had just crashed into was suddenly about to rape her but she didn't care about how fake it looked to other people. She just cared that they looked. Witnesses gathered and she tried to hide her pleasure.

When she was done beating him for all that he was worth, she turned off her video recorder and in a voice that only he could hear said, "I got a tape of you attacking me, if I hear something about a hit and run I'm gonna take this shit to the police. Just take this whack ass lil' BMW down the street and leave me alone."

With him still on the ground, she got back into her car, and swung the door outward so that it hit him slam in the forehead. He fell on his back and she closed her door. Instead of going on about her business, Yvonna's evil ass rammed into the back of the man's car breaking his bumper. When she backed up and pulled out, she smiled at the damage she'd caused. Once far enough from the scene, she called Bricks.

"Are you aight?" he asked excitedly. "Were you hurt?"

"Fuck that! Let me tell you something, you don't know nothin' 'bout me bein' a mother. I'm a damn good mother. I love my daughter, and everything I do including keepin' time wit' you to get rid of this nigga is for her. So don't ever disrespect me again."

"When you comin' to pick her up? 'Cause I'm not 'bout to argue wit' you 'bout this shit. I got somewhere to be in a hour."

All the arguing in the world didn't change the fact that she had to pick up Delilah before going to her meeting in Virginia. But who could she get to watch her at such short notice? She would rather kill Penny then to ask her to watch her baby again. And Ming was out of town. Then she remembered her sister Jesse and smiled. She hadn't talked to her since she'd been home, but she was sure she'd love to do it. She had been spending a lot of time with her niece while Yvonna was hospitalized and they had a good bond.

"I'll be on my way in twenty minutes to get Delilah. And don't worry, I won't ask you for anything else again."

She pulled over on the side of the road and tried to remember Jesse's number. Her nails tapped on the steering wheel and suddenly, she thought she saw Martin Lawrence walk across the street. Remembering what happened at the club with Bricks she closed her eyes tightly opened them back and again Martin Lawrence was there.

"Please stop," she said to herself. "Please...please...please stop."

Pressing her fingers firmly against her eyes, she counted...one...two...three. When she reopened her eyes he was gone, and she remembered Jesse's number.

"I don't know why you callin' that bitch!" Gabriella said angrily, "She doesn't care 'bout you or that kid."

What bothered her about Gabriella's comment wasn't that she expressed loathe toward her sister, but that if Gabriella felt hate for Jesse, that somewhere deep inside herself, she felt hate toward her sister too. After all, she had learned in the institution that Gabriella was only an extension of who she really was and what she really felt.

"Shut up! I love my sister!" She said rubbing her throbbing temples. A passing driver looked as she talked to herself in her car.

"That bitch doesn't love you!"

"Go away!" Yvonna screamed. "Go away! I don't need

you!"

"Mam, are you okay?" A lady asked passing her on the street.

"Bitch, get your sloop footed ass away from my car!"

The woman ran away and since Gabriella was gone, she called Jesse. "Hello?" Jesse said when Yvonna called her.

"Jesse...it's me, Yvonna."

"Hey! Where have you been?" She sounded excited to hear from her and that made her smile. "Is this your new number?"

"Yeah. Lock it in your phone too."

"I already did!" she said happily. "I called Penny's earlier and she says you aren't staying there anymore. She sounded upset."

"You know how Penny is," Yvonna said softly.

"Oh...well...I was hoping we could get together before I go back to school tomorrow." She said skipping the subject. "I haven't seen you in months."

"It's time for you to go back to college already?" Yvonna asked, wishing she had the kind of life that would have allowed her to go to school.

"Actually it's not. But I have a new roommate in my dorm room in UCLA and I want to make sure I keep an eye on my stuff when she moves in. But I want to see my big sister before I leave. Hope I'm not being too mushy."

It was still weird to Yvonna that she could hold a conversation with her sister despite their violent past. After all, she was the reason Jesse had to wear a prosthetic limb.

"You not being too mushy. Maybe we can see each other before you leave tomorrow."

"I'd like that! Yvonna," Jesse paused, "How have you been? Have things been working out with your treatment?"

"Yeah. I'm not having any issues like I use to," she said despite seeing Gabriella sitting in the passenger seat earlier.

"And I'm not violent either," she continued with her lies, despite drop kicking a man a few miles back.

Yvonna could hear Jesse smile through the phone. "I'm glad to hear that."

"Jesse, I have an important meeting to go to today, and I can't take Delilah with me. Do you mind watchin' your niece for me? For a couple hours?"

"Sure...but I'm sure Penny could do it for you."

"I'm asking you," Yvonna said, not wanting her to know that there was tension between she and Penny. "I figure this will give you some time to be with your niece while helping me out at the same time."

"No problem. I'm at the old house. I'll see you when you get here."

Yvonna jotted to Bricks house, grabbed her baby and left without a word to him. The more they fought, and he stayed, the more she felt a connection toward him, and that scared her most of all. Once she dropped Jesse off, she was on her way to Virginia when her phone rang.

"Hello," Yvonna said in an irritated tone. "Who is this?"

"You shouldn't use this phone if you wanna live. You really made him angry by killing his cousin. Please protect your family and go as far away as possible."

Click.

"Hello...hello!" She screamed looking at the phone. "Tell me who you are?"

It was too late; once again, the caller was gone.

DOWN TO THE WIRE

Jona, Peter, Guy, Lily and Terrell met at the usual motel to discuss the new details on Yvonna.

"So what's up?" Lily asked nonchalantly, "This thing has caused us too much time and we want to round it up."

"I found out a lot." Terrell said convincingly. "And it's changed my stance on this whole situation. I don't think she's the monster we made her out to be."

"You're kidding right?" Lily asked looking at the others. Their eyes told Terrell that conversations occurred about him behind his back.

"I'm very serious, Lily. This girl has gone through a lot."

"And we haven't?" She laughed. "So tell us, what has the good doctor learned that will make us forget about all of the people she's killed? And that our own lives might be in danger?"

"Before I go any further, does anybody remember the name Penny Hightower?"

"Penny Hightower?" Guy repeated looking at his partner Peter.

"Yeah." Terrell confirmed.

"That's the woman who Yvonna was staying with before she turned herself into the institution. She's like her guardian or somethin'. Why?"

"I knew I recognized the name." Terrell said in validation remembering her at Yvonna's first court trial. "Can you speak to her? It seems there's a connection between Gabriella and Yvonna"

"You know they took us off the case." Guy said. "They hired some new detectives who believe Yvonna isn't involved in any of this. So unless we just make a house call, there's no way we can justify to our superiors why we're even talking to her. She could file a harassment case and we'll lose our badges."

"He's right. I say the less people we bother the better. That way when we do decide to move on this, we won't have awakened a bunch of witnesses."

Terrell scratched his head, placed his hand on his hip and paced the room. "What if I met with her alone? I can pretend I'm asking about information on an old patient or something like that. I won't even elude to Yvonna...just Gabriella."

"Look...I already said it's not a good idea," Peter said seriously. His brows creased. "So don't push it."

"Is that all you got?" Lily questioned. "You've wasted all this time only to tell us Penny's name and a possible association?"

"Yes. I mean...no. I found out that Penny and the pastor from the church where Gabriella was last seen, were together at one point and time. And Penny was also in charge of some place where Gabriella was being housed and abused." Their expressions remained stone and he could tell they needed more. "Anyway, the pastor's oldest son and Gabriella were close. It was during the same time Yvonna was in the picture.

"From what I understand, Gabriella and Yvonna were in some kind of children's hell hole together. My informant, who was later killed after I met with him, said that Gabriella was some kind of child hero in this place. It's probably why Yvonna developed the Gabriella personality to protect her because she was that to her when they were kids. So if I can find out what Yvonna went through, maybe I could prevent her from killing in the future and we won't need to kill her."

"Wait...so you want to save her instead of killing her?" Guy asked.

"What I'm saying is that I think we should hold off," Terrell said, "I think we should not make a move until I find out more information."

Lily laughed and shook her head. "I told you all," she said looking at the others. "He has no intention in moving on this matter."

"Don't you get it? Somewhere out there, some place exists which abuses children. We can be heroes if we can get Yvonna to recall where this place is." He paused looking around the room.

"I'm not interested in being a hero! I'm interested in living." Lily interjected.

"But maybe I...I can...get her some therapy or something," he said to no one in particular. "And maybe I can put her under hypnosis and find out more information. I don't know," he said shrugging his shoulders. "I do know that until we find out what happened in that place, we should hold off."

Lily walked up to him and left a few spaces in between them in case he wanted to strike her. "We've decided to kill Yvonna in two days. With or without you."

"What?" Terrell asked with great confusion.

"You...discussed this without me?" Their betrayal hurt him.

"We had no choice," Peter said. "You're roaming around here like some fuckin' super psychiatrist and forgetting what matters. I'm sorry, Terrell, but I haven't been able to sleep since I found out she was home. And already, people are dying."

"What are you talking about?"

"Treyana's husband, Avante, was found strangled to death in his home. They think it's some kind of sick sexual lunatic but I think not. I'm sure it was Yvonna. She probably chased him down because of his involvement with Treyana and she won't let up until everyone who knows anything is dead." Guy continued. "Including us."

"So we're sorry, man, but we have to move on this." Peter added. "We can waste no more time."

"I'm begging you," Terrell pleaded with deep sympathy in his eyes, "don't kill her yet. Let me talk to her. If I see one inkling of murder in her eyes I'll kill her myself. I promise you."

"Terrell, just stop! You're making yourself look ridiculous!" Jona screamed getting up from her sitting position on the bed. Normally she was quiet in the meetings but the thought of losing Terrell because of his sick insatiable desire to save Yvonna was too much to bear. "I don't feel comfortable either with her being home. And I didn't want to tell you this but in my meeting with her, she told me she would kill me. Soon."

"What?" he said, his face screwed up. "You never told me anything like that?"

"Yes I did," she lied.

"No you didn't," he said sternly. "I would've remembered that. I think you said something about her being jealous or some shit like that. But that was the extent of it."

"You were so wrapped up in finding her that you haven't paid me much attention lately," she said giving the group too much information on their relationship.

Terrell looked at her in disgust. He knew she was lying but he also knew the others believed her. If he gave her a piece of his mind, he'd only succeed at making himself look more ridiculous and she'd win their favor.

"I didn't mean to upset you, Jona," he said softly, "I'm just saying something that important, I would've remembered."

"Do you care more about Yvonna than your own fiancé?" Lily asked. "How cold can you really be?"

"Of course I care about her!" He said looking at Jona who was now sobbing. "That's...that's not what I'm saying."

"Then it's settled, the bitch dies in two days," Lily said rubbing Jona's back who had suddenly fallen to pieces on the bed. "With or without you she dies."

SPLASH

"Oh shit! I think she's drowning!" A young white man yelled as he sat by the poolside on a green lawn chair. "Somebody go get her!"

"I'm not fuckin' wit' that sick bitch. She said she wanted to get in there, let her stay in there." An older black man said before pulling on a glass weed pipe.

"Are ya'll gonna get her or not?" A red haired white female asked as she stood by the sliding door connected to the pool. "Ya'll brought her here ya'll go get her. I don't want the cops in my house on account of a dead bitch."

When no one moved, she decided she had to go save her. Diving into the water fully clothed, she pulled Yvonna out and placed her on the poolside. The men realizing she was really hurt rushed to her side. The black man performed CPR until water escaped her mouth. When she opened her eyes, three people she didn't recognize were standing over top of her.

"Are you okay, Gabriella?" The black man asked. Yvonna recognized him as Jeff, the man who sold her the

Lidocaine.

"Where am I?"

"You're at my house." Jeff said. "Are you okay?"

"Yeah," she said coughing up more water. "How long have I been here?"

"Since yesterday." He said.

Yvonna hopped up and looked at herself. She was wearing a red bathing suit and she couldn't remember a thing. The longer she went without medication, the more reckless she became. The last thing she recalled was meeting with Jeff and making the fake cocaine with mashed speed pills and the Lidocaine combined. The next thing she knew, she was laying by the poolside with strange lips on top of hers.

"What happened?"

"Bitch you know what happened!" The white female said lunging toward her. The men held her back. "You came with my cousin Chris over here, and instead of being with him, you decided you wanted to fuck my husband Jeff. You're a drunk who can't handle her liquor and I want you out of here."

Yvonna could've screamed on her but she didn't have the time. Besides, a whole day had gone by and she hadn't remembered.

"When did I get here?"

"Yesterday. It's now twelve in the afternoon."

"Oh, no! I have to leave!" Yvonna said sitting up straight.

"Are you sure you're okay?" Jeff asked. "You been drinking and smoking weed all night."

"She said she has to go!" His wife yelled. "So I want her out of here."

Yvonna hustled into the house, grabbed her things which she saw on the kitchen table and was out the door.

Chris, who resembled Matt Damon followed behind her. He jogged to the driver side window before she pulled off.

"Look, I know you're not going to call me, but if you ever need anything, I'd like to hear from you again." He said handing her a piece of paper with his number on it. She took it and threw it in her console.

"Drive safe." He said backing away from the window.

Before she left she said, "Hey...did we...you know?"

"Have sex?" He laughed.

"Yes."

"No...I wanted to but you didn't."

"Well did I sleep with your cousin?"

"Heck no!" he laughed. "Rose would've killed you."

"Imagine that," Yvonna said realizing if Gabriella took over like she was sure she did, that killing her would be the last thing she'd be able to do. "I'll be in touch."

They were fifteen minutes in the drive to meet Yao's New York customer and there was tension between them and Yvonna knew why. When she first went over Ming's, he was upset because she was thirty minutes late. But what could she do? She was crazy drunk and high and lost track of time. The damage was done.

"What do you really want?" Yvonna asked when she noticed he was staring at her. She was driving her car. "And why are you always staring at me?"

"Which question do ya want me ta answer first?" He said slyly.

"The stares. It creeps me out."

"I stare at ya because ya a scheming temptress."

"A scheming temptress?"

"Yes. You love controlling tings don't ya? Love knowing all the plays before they're made. Well ya should know, my dear that ya can't control everyting and everybody."

"Who are you to tell me what I can't do?" She asked rolling her eyes.

"I'm just a man who wants ta get into your head."

"Well you should un-interest yourself with me." She said looking over at him as she maneuvered down the road.

"Ya telling me not ta interest myself with ya won't do," he said turning his head to look out the window. "It won't do at all."

Yvonna felt his mysterious stares and hated that she felt stimulated sexually. His accent. His body. Everything about her best friend's boyfriend was turning her on but she despised him at the same time. "Why are you here?"

He smiled and said, "I suggested ta the lady Ming that she invite you along. That way we can have some alone time."

"What's up wit' you and Bricks? Why did you cut the package?"

"He told ya that?" He laughed.

"Yeah."

"I cut it because I wanted ta. I take what I want." He admitted that he didn't play fair and allowed it to roll off his shoulders. "Don't look at me that way, girl," he smiled, "ya do tings ya want because ya want ta all the time. Don't ya?"

"Look, Darcus, you bad news." She said trying to focus on the road. "And I don't know why I know you are but I just do. So let's just get this over with, and stay out of each other's paths...okay?"

"Ya don't get it, Yvonna." He smirked. "I came here for ya and I'm not leaving without ya."

"What does that mean?"

"You'll find out soon enough. For now, I'll leave ya to ya peace."

SNOOPIN' AROUND

"I'm surprised you wanted to see me today," Jona said to Terrell as she sat at her desk. "I missed you so much even though we live together I don't see you at all." Terrell sat across from her at her office.

"I know, baby. After I heard what Yvonna said to you at the meeting yesterday, it made my stomach sick. I was so busy worrying about her that I neglected you." Under the soft light he looked even more handsome.

Jona walked from around her desk and moved toward him. Standing above him, she slowly dropped to her knees like a child and caressed his hands. At first she felt him tug away from her, but she willingly let him go. "I love you so much, Terrell. All I want to do is make you happy. Sometimes I feel like I can't compete with her though. Like you still love her." She gently pushed his legs apart. "Can I make you happy now?"

In shock, he allowed her to unfasten his pants. In their entire relationship, she had never given him head. But for some reason, today was different. Removing his dick from his pants, she stroked him until he was thick and hard.

When he was just right, she placed him into her mouth giving his shaft long wet strokes like it was candy.

"Mmmmmm," he moaned pawning the back of her head, "you feel so good."

"I love you," Jona was risking getting caught by her boss since she was at work, but she didn't care. "I love you so much." Licking the sides of his penis she then tickled the tip of his smooth bronze helmet with her warm tongue.

"Don't stop," he demanded. "Just like that."

At it for a while, she was surprised he hadn't cum because he was normally a two-minute brother. Five minutes passed and he still hadn't reached an orgasm. The truth was, he was no longer attracted to her.

"Does it feel good?" she asked looking up at his closed eyes hopefully.

"Yeah...real good, baby." He said struggling to reach that place.

"I want to taste that cum," she begged doing a better job of pleasing him, "I want to swallow your love cream. Can you give it to me baby? Can you let me taste it?" she continued jerking his penis in quick swift motions while sucking at the same time. "Come all in my hot warm mouth."

Although he was enjoying it, he still hadn't reached the spot. And then she said, "Do I suck your dick better than Yvonna?" He opened his eyes and looked down at her.

"What...yes...yes, baby." He said pumping into her mouth. He was confused but didn't let it stop his motions.

"Be honest," she spit on it making it wet and licked the sides.

"You can pretend I'm her if you want to," she invited.

"W...what?"

"I said you can pretend I'm her if you want to. I want you to call me Yvonna."

"For real?" he asked as he looked down on her. "You not going to be mad?"

"No," she said slightly hurt he didn't refuse at least once. "You can do whatever you want. Just don't leave me."

Closing his eyes, he pumped into her mouth and said, "Suck my dick, Yvonna. Suck that shit!"

Jona kept her mouth open but the extra work she was putting in a few moments earlier had ceased. After all, she wasn't going to give him her best head job ever, only for Yvonna to receive credit. But what she didn't know was that he imagined she was Yvonna every time they fucked, he just never said it out loud.

He grabbed the back of her head and said, "Damn, Yvonna. That shit feel so good. I'm about to cum! I'm about to cum on them pretty lips of yours. You want that shit don't you?"

Damn he's going all the way with it. She thought.

A tear fell down her face but Terrell could care less, his feelings were finally out of the bag. He was still in love with Yvonna and there was nothing she could do about it. With a few more swift hard pumps, Terrell's dick touched the back of her throat causing her to gag. He didn't care. He kept his hold of her head until he spurted all of his cream into her throat. Only then did he release the death grip he had on her.

When she finished, he stood up and said, "Damn, baby. That shit was hot! I wasn't even expecting that treat when I came to see you." He fastened his pants.

She swallowed the clump of cum in her throat and said, "I'm glad you liked it."

"I loved it. But before you get comfortable, can you

get me something' to drink?" You wore me out."

"Sure...but when I come back, can we talk?" She asked standing up.

"Yes, whatever you want," he said trying to get rid of her.

The moment she left, he ran through her desk drawers looking for Penny's address. He knew she had it somewhere because she was Yvonna's doctor. Within five minutes of searching, he grew frustrated until he touched her keyboard. The computer was locked but he knew that the letters, T...E...R...R...E...L...L, would allow him the access needed. He was right. Luckily for him Penny's address was in a folder marked Yvonna Harris on Jona's desktop. He jotted the information down and was about to leave until Jona walked into her office and caught him red-handed.

He looked up at her and said, "I'm sorry."

"Why, Terrell?" she said dropping the can soda on the floor. "Why is she so important?"

"I don't know." He said folding the piece of paper, which held Penny's address tightly in his hands. "I just wanna make sure she's okay."

"Is it over between us? Can you at least tell me that?"

"I can't answer that question either. Bye, Jona," he said walking out on her.

←——————————————————————→

"Ms. Hightower, can I come in?" Terrell asked after Penny opened the door.

"I knows you," she said softly pointing at him, "but where do I know you from?"

"Please, Ms. Hightower, I just want to ask you a few questions, about Yvonna and I don't want anybody out here hearing our conversation."

Penny's inquisitive stare turned to rage as she

remembered exactly who he was. "You're that doctor. The one who testified for Yvonna in her first case."

"Yes. I was her doctor."

"You were also her lover or somethin' too right?" Penny persisted.

"Yes...Yvonna and I were together at one time."

Penny opened the door wider, "Come on in. And have a seat."

He walked inside and looked around, "Is Yvonna here? I really have to talk to her."

"I haven't seen Yvonna in a few days." She frowned. "I don't know what to say about that chile anymore. Just washed my hands of her a few days ago."

"Why?"

"She's not a good mother. I'll leave it at that. I called Jona to give her my opinion on the hold thing, course she don't seem to want to hear what I gots to say."

"What exactly did you tell Jona?"

"Yvonna was 'spose to be stayin' here, as a condition of her release...but she ain't been here. Now I been raisin' the baby, and I wants to keep it like that. I don't want no parts of her." She paused. "What's wrong with yous young man?" She asked seeing the disappointment on his face.

"I was hoping to talk to her. And I'm sorry things don't seem to be working out. You seemed to really care about her at the trial."

"Yeah well...some people don't deserve that kind of love, yous understand?"

Terrell couldn't help but remember the conversation he had with the pastor and Dmitry about Penny's unstable traits. Yet she spoke like she was really capable of love but anyone who abused children could not be.

"Yes. I do understand that you can't love everybody. I

found that out earlier today actually. Listen, I found out some information that may be beneficial for Yvonna. Do you know where I can find her?"

"That Chinese chick's house probably. I'm not sure. This wouldn't have nothin' to do with that Gabriella situation now would it?"

"Actually it is." He said surprised she'd known.

"You know yous shouldn't be snoopin around." She said looking at him sternly. "Just leave well enough alone. I'm warnin' you for your own good young man. Some boats don't need to be rocked."

"What...I...I don't understand."

"Yous a doctor and that means you got a degree and it also means you smart enough to know what I'm sayin'. It's 'cause of you that boy Dmitry not here no more. We don't like our business known. And you could be next."

Terrell remembered how scared he was when he first found out Yvonna suffered from schizophrenia, but nothing she'd ever done, prepared him for the woman he was standing before that day.

"Are you still running that place? Are more kids there that I don't know about?" He asked feeling great discomfort because of prying.

She laughed and said. "This thing is way bigger than your young mind could conceive. If this thing gets out, a lot of money is lost and a lot of people get hurt. Go away. 'Cause you 'bout to taste a drink you can't swallow. The only reason yous still alive is because you don't know nothin'. Don't mess that up. Do I make myself clear?" She advised giving him a cold glare.

"Yes. Painfully clear."

Penny walked to the door and opened it, "Don't come back around here. If yous know what's good for yous."

BIG BROTHER

"I can't believe it!" Melvin said shaking his head. "I can't believe you actually got back up wit' that bitch again. And then you let her interfere wit' business? Where ya head at lil bro?" Forty five year old Melvin was extremely close and overprotective of his only brother Bricks.

"It's not even what you think. Shawty ain't put me in this shit, that nigga Swoopes did."

"But what about this shit wit' Cameo?"

"That wasn't her either. But if Cameo gonna let the nigga Darcus interfere wit' our business knowin' I don't fuck wit' the nigga either, then maybe we should look for another player." Bricks said sitting on the sofa drinking a beer. "That's some bitch shit you know that Melvin."

"Did you talk to Cameo yet?"

"Yeah…we met yesterday. And he was actin' a little off, I'm tellin' you. But that shit ain't got nothin' to do wit' Yvonna."

Melvin looked down at his younger brother and sat across from him. He folded his hands together and gripped them tightly. "You really feelin' this bitch ain't you?"

"Come on man, don't call her a bitch no more?" He said through tight lips. "I'd appreciate that, brah."

Bricks' response answered his question. He sighed and said, "What's our next move?"

"Well like I said, I met with Cameo yesterday, as far as he's concerned we still doin' business. But I figure we start gettin' a little somethin' from Mom's every now and again, just to open that connection. If Cameo stops trippin', we continue as is...but if not, we take our business elsewhere. Point is, it's plenty other places to get that from."

"Mom's deals in prescriptions though. We ain't got no market for that shit."

"That's just his bread and butter, but slim got access to everything, Melvin. Trust me. He be on that prescription shit 'cause it's easy to get and the market is wide open. But he can get it all and he been tryin' to deal wit' girl. He know a couple of niggas from the DM (Dominican Republic) who wanna work wit' him. He just don't have no way to move it. That's where we come in. If we have to."

Just when he said that Mom's called. "This the nigga right here," he said answering his cell phone. "Hello."

"What's up, fam, I hear them peoples still on vacation." Mom's said.

He meant that he heard Swoopes was still alive.

"That's not a problem. We got the information we needed from you, so his trip is not gonna be too much longer. In three weeks everything will be lovely. But look...I need to meet you before then."

"Mmmmmm," Mom's moaned. "It sounds like whatever you wanna talk to me about, may be beneficial for both of us. When do we meet?"

"How 'bout tomorrow."

"Tomorrow it is."

He hung up the phone and Melvin shook his head. "Lil bro, I know you run the family business, and you been doin' a good job so far. I just don't feel right about changin' up or this drama. I say you dump that broad, make amends with Cameo, and restore business back to usual."

Just when he said that, the phone rang again. "Hello."

Bet was softly sobbing on the line and he figured she'd gotten the call he feared. That Kendal was murdered.

"What's up, Bet?" He sighed. "You got word on that?"

"They said if you don't meet them today, they gonna kill my baby. Somebody killed his cousin, and he thinks it was you," she continued. Bricks knew it was Yvonna and he finally understood she wasn't the sweet little girl he hoped for. That made her dangerous. "I'm askin' you a lot. To put your life in danger for my son, but right now, you all I got. I don't want to lose him, Bricks. Not again," she said softly.

It was the first time he'd heard her refer to Kendal as her son. Ever since Kendal's, whose birth name was Mitchel K Blake, wife had caught him in bed with another man, which resulted in him trying to kill himself, he had never been the same. When he survived the coma his suicide attempt left him in, he didn't feel like lying about who he really was. Mitch changed his name to Kendal and decided to live the life he wanted, as a woman. At first Bet fought with Kendal but after awhile she saw it was no use and that she had to except that her son was no longer a man, but a woman.

On her first day of living as a woman, Kendal met Bricks at a Redskins game in Landover, but Bricks wasn't head over heels about her and the very thing that drew him to her, also pushed him away. Bricks thought her feminine features were exaggerated, and that something wasn't right. Her extra large breasts and rounded hips looked manufactured and fake. Everything was big on Kendal but her waist. After a few dates he decided to cut her off. But when he went to her apartment to pick her up and tell her face to face, she was not there, Bet was instead. Kendal had a feeling Bricks was going to cut her off, and asked her mother to speak with him to beg him to stay. That angered Bricks and over drinks, he told Bet that he wasn't feeling Kendal. But surprisingly he was feeling Bet and they had sex that night although Bet never told Kendal. Behind Kendal's back the relationship continued for months. But Kendal never gave up and Bet begged Bricks to keep their relationship a secret.

After awhile, Kendal's behavior grew physical and she would hurt herself for attention. With Bet being out of town most times dropping off drug packages for a few customers, she was afraid to leave Kendal alone and asked Bricks to take her in on those weekends. Bricks didn't mind keeping Chomps but letting Kendal hang out at his place was out of the question. But she persisted saying ultimately she was worried about Chomps safety. Against his judgment, he agreed to let them stay for a while. And the weekends turned into weeks and the weeks turned into months with his bond for Chomps deepening.

One day Bricks went to the restroom without knocking and saw Kendal pissing standing up straight. He went ballistic and threatened both Bet and Kendal's lives. For days he was consumed by rage and would go around the house punching at the walls. Had it not been for Chomps, neither Kendal nor Bet would've stayed with him after that. And that was exactly two weeks before he ran back into Yvonna.

"Bet, I feel fucked up about Kendal. But there ain't shit I can do about that situation right now."

Bet's voice sounded desperate but calm. Almost too calm. And when he heard Chomps' cries in the background, chills ran through his spine.

"Bet...what's up wit' Chomps?" he asked standing up. Silence. "Bet...what's up wit' Chomps? Why he screaming like that?"

"What...who...is Chomps?" Bet said forgetting she even had her grandson.

"Fuck you mean who is Chomps?" He bellowed. "He's your baby! I mean...your grandchild."

"Oh...I...don't know why he's crying. I...forgot to feed him I guess."

"When was the last time you fed him?"

"Two days ago."

"Which hotel are you in?"

"Holiday Inn," she said, "In Hyattsville"

Bricks grabbed the keys. "Give me your room number. I'm on my way."

KENDAL DOLL

"Where is Yvonna?" Swoopes asked Newbie as she sat naked at the computer station in the living room. He liked to keep her that way, in case he wanted to use her sexually.

"I don't know...she has the phone turned off." She said examining the computer screen. "She hasn't turned it on again."

Through stiff lips he said, "She been keepin' that shit off a lot lately. I wonder what's up wit' that."

"I don't know why," she responded, her face flushed purple. "What you want me to do?"

"Fuck!" Swoopes said banging the wall with his fist. "Just keep checkin'! Don't take your eyes off of that screen."

Just when he said that, the smell in the kitchen where Crystal cooked his meal caused his stomach to churn. When she finally came out, she held a plate full of slop in her hands.

"What the fuck you cookin'?" he asked, his nose

turned upward. "This shit stinks!"

Newbie turned around to look at Crystal and waited on her response, so Crystal took her anger out on her. As far as she was concerned, she was the reason Swoopes treated her so badly. "Fuck you lookin' at bitch?! I told you don't put your fuckin' eyes on me!" Newbie quickly turned around and focused back on the screen.

"It's meatloaf and mash potatoes." She raised the plate a little closer to him. "I know it's your favorite, and I was trying to make it for you. The way you like."

Swoopes looked down at the food and said, "Well it ain't the way I like it. Give that shit to that bitch in there." He waved her out of his face. "And when you done, go get me some fried chicken and mumbo sauce from Yums."

Crystal took the plate and opened the second room door in the house. Kendal was tied up, and lying on a mattress on the floor.

"Here...eat," she said sitting in the bed next to her.

"Thank you," Kendal said after Crystal removed her gag. "I appreciate it."

"Don't thank me yet. You got to eat it first," she said with a partial smile. "From what I'm told it might make you sick."

"As hungry as I am, I'll eat anything," Kendal said eating the forkfuls Crystal was feeding her, "Do you think he's going to let me go home?"

Crystal dopped the fork down and paused. "No, Kendal, I don't think he will."

She cried softly but didn't make a sound. "I...I knew he wasn't."

"I'm sorry. I really am. But can you tell me something?"

"Yes."

"Why would you turn yourself over to Swoopes?

He's not somebody who keeps promises. You should've never believed he would help you get back at your friend just because you turned yourself over to him. It was a bad idea. He's very dangerous."

"I guess I could ask you the same thing. Why do you stay with him?"

"Because I loved him from the moment I met him on that pen pal prison site. There's something about him that speaks to me."

"Love speaks to you. I loved Bricks from the moment I laid eyes on him too. But he never got me. Ever."

"Is he gay?"

"You know?" Kendal asked with wide eyes.

"Yes. When I take you to the bathroom, I turn my head, but I still see your thing."

Kendal's face was flushed red. "Does he know?"

"Swoopes doesn't know. He doesn't pay attention to anything but Yvonna."

"That makes two of them. Swoopes and Bricks both. I don't know what is it about that bitch that makes them so obsessive."

"If you know how Bricks feels about her, why get into this thing between Swoopes and Yvonna?"

"I...thought he would come for me. I thought he would feel guilty and I made a big mistake." She said looking into Crystal's eyes. "It's the same sick kind of love you have for Swoopes. Although I know I shouldn't love him and that he doesn't want me, I still do," she paused. "Can you do me a favor? If something happens to me, can you write him a letter for me and tell him how much I love him."

"Sure. What about your baby? Don't you have one?"

"It's a long story. My mother had that baby for my wife when I had one and me. But he doesn't know me any-more than I know him. He'll be fine with my mother. To tell you the truth, I think Bricks loves my son more than he does me." When she heard Swoopes playing with Newbie in the other room and her laughing she said, "Why do you allow him to treat you like that? You know...bring another woman into your home?"

"I can't control him. You see that."

"You have control. More than you know. You just have to show him."

"Fuck are ya'll doin' in there?" Swoopes asked busting in the door interrupting their conversation.

Crystal jumped up from the mattress and said, "Nothing. I was just feeding her." The plate fell off of the side of the bed and hit the floor.

"Well go look at the Sprint tracker with Newbie. That bitch killed Cane and I want her found...tonight."

"Okay...did you want me to feed Kendal first?" she asked hoping to buy her a few more hours to live. She knew he was preparing to murder her soon since it was obvious that Bricks didn't care and wouldn't come for her.

"No. She's eaten all she's gonna need."

Crystal looked at Kendal one last time and mouthed, "I'm sorry."

When she left out of the door, Swoopes sat down on the chair across from the mattress.

"You's a bad bitch. Why that nigga not comin' for you?"

"I don't think I'm the one he cares about."

Swoopes licked his lips and said, "Why? You was so sure he would when you got in touch with me."

"I was wrong."

Swoopes stood up, walked over to the bed and dropped his jeans. After all the abuse he experienced as a child, he seemed to love inflicting the same sexual abuse onto others. "Let me tell you what I'm gonna do. I'ma let you take care of me, and if it's good, I'ma let you leave. Deal?"

"Swoopes, I think there's something you should know about me first."

"I already know," he said with a smile.

She swallowed hard and said, "You know...that I'm a man?" Swoopes stood over Kendal and pushed his dick into her mouth.

"That feels good. Keep it just like that," he told her. "I like that shit."

She felt humiliated but hoped if she did what he wanted, that maybe he would really let her go. Just when he was getting into it, he heard a loud scream in the living room.

"What the fuck?" he yelled, pulling his pants up. He ran into the living room ready to go off on both of them thinking they were fighting again.

"She...stabbed me," Newbie cried dropping to the floor. The puncture hole in her back was deep and long. Blood oozed out of her flesh.

"I'm sorry," Crystal said holding the butcher knife in her hands. "But this is my house."

"If this bitch dies on me," Swoopes told Crystal, "I'ma kill you."

"Then I guess you betta call for help! 'Cause I cut to kill," she said as a tear fell down her face.

"The knife wound missed her main arteries, but I think she'll be okay. Too bad you couldn't catch the muggers though," the doctor said to Swoopes in Newbie's hospital room. "Most strangers would not have stopped. It's a good thing you did."

"Yeah it is fucked up...I mean...it's messed up." He said tripping over his words. "But naw, I could never just leave somebody standin' on the street after somethin' like that. I had to stop."

"And did she get a chance to tell you her name or what happened to her clothes? She can't seem to remember now."

"No, I don't know her name. Her purse was stolen."

"She asked for you. So I'll leave you two alone," he smiled placing his hand on his shoulder. "We should have more young men like you in the world."

That was the first genuine compliment Swoopes had ever received in his life, yet he didn't deserve it. When the doctor dipped behind the white curtain separating the other bed in the room, Swoopes sat on the edge of Newbie's bed and placed his hand on her foot.

"My bad, youngin'. I ain't know my peoples was gonna hit you like that."

Newbie smiled and said, "It's okay. Really."

"She just trippin' about our relationship, she won't pull no shit like that again. I promise you that."

"You not gonna leave me are you? Alone?"

"No." He said looking down at her with kind eyes. For some reason, he was taking to her and he didn't know why. "I'ma just take care of some shit later, and I'll be back to check on you."

"Thank you," she smiled.

When he dipped behind the curtains and moved for the door, Newbie picked up the phone and dialed a number she kept to memory.

She waited impatiently for the person to answer. "Yvonna," she whispered. "I'm the girl who has been calling you. Can we talk?"

"I can't talk, but I can listen," She said. "What do you

want?"

"That phone you're using is being traced by Sprint's tracker system. Swoopes knows where you are when you get there."

"What? What do you mean? How can he trace my number?"

"He's the one who gave you the phone. It's in his girl-friend Crystal's name. Get rid of it, or you gonna die. Oh...and tell Bricks to be careful. He's being set up tonight by Kendal's mother. That's all I can tell you."

"How do I know you telling the truth?"

"Cause I ain't got no reason to lie. I don't like the person he is and he makes me scared." She paused crying. Newbie wished she never left home and now it was too late. "I have been trying to protect you by lying to him about where you are, but now I'm in the hospital and Swoopes has his girlfriend tracing you. She's determined to make him happy so you must be smart. I'm going home and you will never hear from me again. I just wanted to make things right before I left."

"Are you the one who was with him when we shot at his car that night?"

"Yes."

"Thanks for telling me," Yvonna said. "And I hope you make it out of this shit alive. Swoopes is dangerous."

"I'll be fine. Good luck."

When she hung up on Yvonna, she called her father, the preacher. "Dad...I'm sorry for everything I put you through. I got into some things with some people and all I want to do is come home." Newbie cried. "Can I?"

Her father yelled so loudly in the phone it almost hurt her ears, "Thank you God! Thank you!" Newbie smiled when she heard the happiness in his voice. "Yes you can, Alexis. Just tell me where you are, and I'll come get you."

She told him where she was and she prayed Swoopes wouldn't look for her. All she wanted was to go back to school and to be a productive member of society. Unfortunately, her revelation came too late because she hadn't known that Swoopes had never left the room.

"Damn, I knew something was up with you. I just hoped it wasn't true." He said opening the white curtain.

"Please...don't kill me. I want to go home. I won't tell anybody anything."

"You just did."

"I'm sorry. You'll never hear from me again. Ever."

"You should've thought about that before you crossed me," he said taking his gun out of his jacket, snatching the pillow from behind her head and pressing it to her face. With the barrel embedded into the pillow, he pulled the trigger.

UNTAMED HEART

Bet paced the hotel floor until she heard a few raps at her front door. She had been waiting on Bricks ever since he told her he was on his way. Her movements stopped, and her heart beat heavily inside her chest. She was overcome with anxiety and momentarily clasped her hands tightly together before taking a deep breath and dropping them by her sides. Walking quickly to the door, she flung it open and threw a smile on her face. But instead of seeing Bricks, she saw his brother Melvin instead. The look of disappointment showed on her face instantly and she desperately tried to remove it by adding another smile.

"Oh...I wasn't expecting you. Where's your brother?" she asked looking into the hotel's hallway. When she didn't see him she stepped back to let him inside. The black hoody and leather gloves he wore frightened her.

"He couldn't make it," he said after he looked around. It was a suite style and was divided into the bedroom and living room. "So he sent me instead. Am I good enough for you?"

"Oh...uh...yeah. Why wouldn't you be?"

"Where's the kid?" Melvin asked as he surveyed his surroundings. He was in search of anything or anyone out of place. "My brother said he heard him crying. It sounded like something was wrong with him."

"Oh...he's in the bedroom."

He made his way back to the room and he didn't bother to ask if it were okay. Once he saw the kid fast asleep he said, "Look, I have to use your restroom right quick. Where is it?"

"Right over there," she pointed to the hallway door. "What are ya'll gonna do with the baby?"

"Bricks wants me to pick him up," he said as he ran his fingers through one another to make sure the gloves were on tight. And when she turned her head and walked toward the bathroom, he swiped her cell phone off the dresser. "You gotta ask him when you talk to him."

"Oh."

"Look," he stopped before going into the bathroom with the closed door, "I'm not gonna lie, I don't feel too good about all this shit. So if you don't mind, can you go inside first?"

"What? You don't trust me?" she asked doing a horrible job of convincing him he should.

"Go in the fuckin' bathroom," he said with a straight face.

She walked hesitantly into the bathroom and opened the door. "See...it's nothing."

When the door opened, Melvin shoved her inside, and pushed her toward the bathtub. She stumbled inside of it and hit her head on the faucet. Blood poured from her body and into the white tub. Then he yanked the plastic shower curtain down and placed it over her body. "Don't fuckin' move!"

"What are you doin?!"

When she tried to advance, Melvin overpowered her and hit her twice in the face. "Bitch, what you know about this Swoopes shit? Huh?"

"Nothin'. Just that they got my baby."

"You were gonna set my lil brother up?" he asked as he maintained the chokehold he had on her neck.

"No...I don't know what you talkin' about," she said as she clawed at his glove-covered hands.

"Then why that bitch Yvonna call and tell him that?"

"I don't know," she sobbed. "Please don't hurt me."

"If you don't tell me what you told them, I'ma blow your face off. Now what the fuck is up?"

"That he was comin'." She hesitated. "I was supposed to call Swoopes when he got here. That's it. I just wanted Kendal back. I didn't mean to hurt anyone."

He pulled her phone out of his pocket and said, "What's his number?"

"It's in the phone. It was the last number I called."

Melvin quickly dialed the number and when Swoopes answered he said, "What's up dude?" He wasn't concerned that Bricks could be in danger because there were six carloads of his family members parked out front, protecting him. "I'm here with your peoples and she wanna tell you something."

Then he made sure the receiver was directly next to the barrel before he pulled the trigger.

"It's your move." Afterwards he ended the call and left the house with the baby.

LAST STOP

"We need gas," Yvonna said looking at the gauge. "We ain't gonna make it without it."

"I don't know why ya didn't get it back there," Darcus said. "We're running late and we have ta move now."

"Look, we need gas. So I gotta pull over." She said with an attitude before pulling into a truck stop.

Darcus shook his head in irritation and it was the first time he lost his cool. When she pulled up to the gas station, she said, "Can you get me something to drink?" Grabbing her cell phone, she held it tightly in her hand.

"Ya like ta be difficult don't ya?" he paused. "Well I must tell ya, you're wearing on me. And I don't like ta be worn on."

"Please. I'm thirsty and I've been driving all day." Darcus eyed the bag with the weight in it. "It's the least you can do."

"Sure," he said as he scooped the bag up to take it with him. She knew he would. "What ya want to drink?"

"You can leave the bag here."

"What do ya want ta drink?" he said letting it be known he had no intentions of putting it down.

"Are you serious? You're really going to go into the truck stop with a bag full of coke?"

"Ya want something ta drink or not?

"Yeah...buy me a coke." She schemed.

"How convenient," he laughed walking off.

When he left the car, she snapped a picture of him holding the bag, sent it to its destination and quickly cut the phone back off. It took him twenty minutes to return and they were on the road again. About thirty minutes from their destination, she stopped at McDonalds.

"What are ya doing now?" His glare told her she was pushing his buttons.

"I'm going to the bathroom." She said grabbing her purse. "Don't worry, I'll leave the bag. So you can relax."

"I'm not worried. But ya better be. You're messing wit' time that we don't have. Now hurry back," He demanded.

Yvonna paid him no attention as she sashayed toward the bathroom with her purse. When she was done, she walked back to the car, sat on the backseat and threw her jacket over the bag.

"I forgot my tampon. Can you hand me one?"

"What?" He asked looking behind him at her.

"A tampon. It's in my glove compartment."

"What are ya up ta Yvonna? I don't trust ya."

"You know what," she said as she closed the door, pulled down her pants, moved her panties to the side and pulled a bloody tampon from her body, "Here!"

She threw it in his lap and he jumped out of the car and screamed.

"Fuck is wrong wit' ya girl?! Why would ya do someting so tasteless?"

He stomped away from the car in a rage. It was all she needed to replace the bricks in the bag with a concoction she made at Jeff's house. If he came back to the car and tasted it, his tongue would go numb just like the real thing.

She also knew that when he made the drop, he would have a serious problem on his hands when they discovered that the package was fake. And if the New Yorkers didn't kill him, she was sure Ming's uncle Yao would.

"Jamaicans and period blood," she laughed looking at him giving distance from the car as if it were the plague. "So fuckin' stupid."

For that one weakness she spotted when they were at Ming's', he was going to pay with his life.

FOR THE LOVE OF DRAMA

Yvonna sat anxiously in a different parking space from where she dropped Darcus off in New York. He was in the building a few blocks ahead, making the drop, while she sat in the car with the real bags of coke safely in her purse.

After waiting for a few more minutes, she realized she wouldn't be able to hear how things ended up from where she sat. And because curiosity was killing her, she got out of her car, and crept carefully up to the building. Knowing the address, she walked up the stairs and into the hallway. But the moment her foot hit the floor he was on, she heard an angry male's voice.

"Are you tryin' to be funny?"

There was a long pause before she heard Darcus say, "What you talkin' 'bout?"

That was the last she heard before gunfire blasted throughout the tiny apartment and resonated into the hallway. With a smile on her face, she jetted down the stairs and into her waiting car. It had worked! There was no way on earth she could see Darcus walking out of that battle alive. And once she spoke with Ming, she would explain how she found out that Darcus was trying to pass the fake coke off to the connect as real just so he could sell the real bricks himself.

She knew she could convince her of the truth, especially after she presented her with the real bricks. The most important thing was she was rid of a man who she was sure was out to kill her for whatever reason, and that Ming would be safe. At least she hoped so.

A BAD MOVE

"Jesse, I'm sorry I'm late." She said still nervous about what occurred with Darcus. The entire ride from New York to D.C. she thought someone was following her.

"Hey, sis. Is everything okay?"

Jesse backed up into the house she once shared with Jhane, who was believed to have died as a result of the breast cancer she developed, instead of Yvonna's own hands.

"I came for Delilah," Yvonna said looking around the neat home. "Where is she?" She was expecting her to crawl out any minute.

"What...do you mean?" She smiled thinking her sister was joking.

"Stop playing, Jesse. I had a long day. Where's the baby?"

"Penny has her," she said softly realizing something was wrong.

"Jesse...why would you give my baby to Penny?" Her eyes widened and her voice deepened. "What the fuck were you thinking?!" It was the first time she'd yelled at her sister since they were kids.

"Yvonna, slow down," she said with her prosthetic arm extended out in front of her. The thought of all the people Yvonna killed ran through her mind. "You picked Delilah up yesterday. Remember?"

"No I didn't." she said trying to maintain her composure. "I dropped her off and I didn't come back until now."

"Yes you did. You said you needed more time away and that Delilah was slowing you down. You said you wanted Penny to have her and you came with an older black man and a white kid about my age."

"I know you not gonna let this bitch play you are you?" Gabriella appeared. "She gave your kid to that bitch and she tryin' to pass it off on you."

As Yvonna listened to Gabriella's voice, she grew angrier. Suddenly she felt like Jesse *was* trying to make her think that she was crazy. All the thoughts of how she betrayed her by testifying in court against her reentered her mind.

Yvonna walked carefully up to her and said, "You in on it ain't you? You don't want me to have my baby and you trying to make me think I'm crazy."

"What?" Jesse asked backing up into a wall. "I would never do anything like that to you. I love you, Yvonna. But you did pick the baby up. Honest."

"Stop lyin'. You don't think I'm good enough do you?" Yvonna's throat felt like it was closing and her forehead started to sweat. The longer she'd gone without her medication, the harder it was to control her delusions.

"Yvonna, I would never do anything to harm you," she said frightened. "Please don't hurt me again."

Yvonna had stepped so close to her sister that there

was no place else for Jesse to move. And then Yvonna looked into Jesse's eyes. This was her family. This was her baby sister, and she couldn't hurt her anymore.

"I gotta go," Yvonna said running toward the door.

"Yvonna, please. Stay and talk to me." She cried. "I love you."

"I know you do," Yvonna said turning around to look at her. "And that's why I'm gonna leave. So I can protect you...from me."

HEART LOCK

Quietly, Melvin drove Bricks and Chomps to the house. Bricks sat in the passenger seat and looked through the side view mirror. It seemed as if the whole block was trailing behind him. He was thankful he had a family so deep but at the time, all he could think about was Yvonna and he wondered if she was okay.

"What's on your mind, bro?" Melvin asked as he maneuvered on the road ahead of him.

"What?" Bricks asked looking over at him.

"Your ass ain't even listenin' to me," he shook his head. "I said what's on your mind?"

Bricks looked behind him at Chomps who was fast asleep in a car seat. "Nothin'. Just wondering how long Tina gonna help me take care of this kid. I'ma need her help, at least until I find out what I'ma do wit' him."

"You sure you should be taking care of the kid? I mean, I did kill its mother. What if the police start snoopin' 'round?"

"It won't be too bad because Bet made me a

guardian after Kendal signed over her parental rights to her. Bet stayed out of town and Kendal couldn't watch him all the time. So when Chomps got sick one day when Bet was out of town, I told her she had to give me guardianship if she was goin' to leave him with me 'cause them fuckin' doctors wouldn't let me authorize his treatment at the hospital. So technically I'm legally his caregiver. Kendal wasn't tryin' to be bothered with this kid."

"When are you going to tell me what's up with Kendal?" Melvin probed.

"It's nothin', man," Bricks frowned. "It's too involved. Let's just say nothing happened between me and that bitch but I'll take her secret to my grave."

"Whatever," Melvin said irritated that his own brother didn't trust him enough to tell him about the controversy that surrounded Kendal. "You shoulda let me fuck her."

"Trust me, I did you a favor," Bricks laughed. "But back to Chomps. I just can't see the kid goin' into the system. Think about how our Moms did us by fuckin' wit' that crack. That foster care system is some shit man and I don't wanna see that shit happen to him."

"I agree," he said remembering the hard times they experienced trying to stay together in the system.

"Yeah. They should just let kids get emancipated."

Melvin looked over at him and said, "You don't think it's weird? For you to be so close to him?"

"What you tryin' say, man?" Bricks snapped.

"I'm sayin, maybe you should get a girlfriend before you get a baby." Melvin paused when he took into account his own words. "Or maybe you already got one."

Bricks looked over at him and smiled. "Naw, I'm single."

"You fightin' wars on account of this chick. You not hardly single."

He laughed and said, "I don't know why I can't shake her. It fucks me up."

"Maybe you like drama."

"Naw...but she gets me, and my lifestyle," he smiled. "Man you should've seen shawty buckin' at them niggas who was firin' at us the day we first hooked up. That's my kinda bitch." He got quiet. "But then there's some other shit she just hit me wit' that I don't know how to handle. It threw me for a loop."

"Like what?"

Bricks didn't want to add more reasons for Melvin not to like Yvonna so he posed a hypothetical question instead of saying she had schizophrenia.

"If you knew someone, who had an illness, would you stick by them?"

"She got that monkey on her back do she?" He asked with wide eyes referring to her having AIDS.

"Fuck no!" he said looking at him crazy. "It's some other shit, *not* sexually related."

Melvin pulled up in front of Bricks house and parked. His cousins parked one by one and he waved at them as they walked into their houses. "I'ma be real," Melvin started, "you know I don't like the chick."

"Yea, you made that clear."

"No listen," he said extending his hand out in front of him before dropping it down. "I don't like her but I know for a fact you do. So if I fucked wit' somebody as much as you fuck wit' her, and found out she had an illness *not* sexually related," he smiled, "yea...I'd stick by her."

"Thanks, man."

"No problem. But have you been able to get in contact with her since she called you about the set up? 'Cause I know for a fact this dude not gonna let her get away easy. He kickin' over a lota stones to find her. You gotta be careful. And I don't want you goin' out at all without the family."

"I know. And I can't reach her. Every time I call that phone, it goes straight to voicemail. We got into somethin' yesterday so I figure she may be mad at me. I hope she's okay though."

"She fine, nigga." He said mushing his head. "Now get your sucka for love ass out my car. I'm hungry and I know you got somethin' in there to eat."

"What I look like your bitch? You betta cook somethin' yourself."

"Fuck it," Melvin said getting out, while Bricks grabbed the baby. "Tell Forty and them the pizza man gonna be comin' on the block so they can let him pass. And you ain't gettin' shit either!"

"Shiiiiit. I bet I get one of them slices too," Bricks laughed.

"We'll see about that."

TO LOVE A SNAKE

Yvonna banged heavily on Penny's door as her feet beat the concrete. In her purse sat the knife she had all intentions of using if things got out of hand.

"Yvonna, I'm glad yous finally home, chile." She said hugging her. Yvonna pushed her away. "Is everything okay?"

"Penny," she paused looking up at her with hateful eyes, "Give me my baby back. You've got five minutes."

"I'm afraid I can't do that, you see, yous were only released because yous were stayin' here with me. If yous leave, the baby has to stay where it will be safe and I'm gonna have to let them peoples know the truth. Anyway, you brought her here yesterday saying you didn't want her anymore. So what's the problem?"

"Penny, I'm tryin'," Yvonna said as a warm tear melted against her skin, "not to hurt you. Now you've been good to me in the past, and I appreciate it. But if you don't bring my baby down them steps, I might murder you right here and right now."

"Is that what you think, chile?" Penny said stepping onto the porch. Her large burly body pushed against Yvonna's knocking her back a few steps. "Do you really think yous could hurt any parts of me and that I'd let you? Why don't you try it?" She said with her fist nestled into her hips. "Try puttin' your hands on me."

Yvonna's mind told her not to harm her because she could lose her baby. But, she also knew she could carve 100 pounds of fat off of her before she even knew what happened. Right when she decided to stab and ask questions later, she heard Terrell's voice behind her.

"Penny, I need you to bring the baby downstairs," he said walking up the steps. He had been sitting in the car waiting on Yvonna to show up to pick up the baby.

Her face frowned as she pushed Yvonna aside to meet him at the bottom of the steps. "What do you gots to do with this? I told you about meddlin' didn't I?"

"I got everything to do with it," he said stepping back. Nobody wanted Penny to close up on them. "Yvonna is in my custody and therefore I will be in charge of her and Delilah," he lied holding tightly to a blank piece of paper in his hand. "So bring the baby out of the house now, or I'll have to call the authorities."

"You're going to wish yous never fucked with me," Penny said disappearing into the house.

Yvonna had never seen Penny so angry and she realized there was more to her than met the eye.

I'll explain everything later," Terrell said looking at Yvonna. "I'm so sorry for everything you've been through too. I really am."

Yvonna's mind raced, and she was confused at everything happening around her. She wondered why Penny was changing for the worse and why Terrell was there to save her. Fifteen minutes later, Penny came out with

Delilah.

She gave the baby a kiss and said, "I'll be back for you."

"What the fuck is that supposed to mean?" Yvonna asked. But it was too late, Penny had slammed the door in her face.

"Come with me," Terrell said, "I have a lot to tell you. And it's not safe around here."

"I don't remember, Terrell. I don't remember a lot about my childhood."

"I figured you didn't. But maybe in the future, we can try hypnosis again. It worked for you in the past."

"Whatever," she said shrugging her shoulders. "For real, I don't think I wanna know."

"But it's important, Yvonna. There may be some other children who are going through what you are. As a matter of fact, I'm sure of it." When Terrell saw her hesitancy he said, "Let me take you somewhere. Just for a little while."

"Let's go," she said shrugging her shoulders.

A half an hour later, they were in front of a church. The brick structure looked familiar but she couldn't be sure. "Why are we here?"

"Have you been here before?" Terrell asked parking.

"No. But for some reason, I hate churches." She seemed to disappear into her thoughts before she focused back on Terrell. "I always have. You know how some people gravitated toward crosses? Well I ran the other way. But I don't know why." She said looking at him. "Why are we here anyway? And at night?"

"When you were institutionalized this time, I wanted to know why you took on personalities of people you...well...killed."

"You don't know what you talkin' about!" she said with an attitude. There's no proof that I killed anyone."

"Listen, I'm not here to judge you, Yvonna. I just want to help you. I'm on your side. But I do need to know. Did you kill Avante?"

She swallowed hard and said, "No."

"I knew it," he smiled.

"But why are you here? One minute you don't like me, and the next minute you dating my doctor. Why should I trust you?"

"Yvonna, I never hated you. Ever. Think about it. The last time I spoke to you personally, I testified in your defense in court. Does that sound like a man who hates you? Even after you stole my money I was still there for you when you needed me. And I'm trying to be here for you now. Allow me to."

"I'm listenin'," she said softly.

"Gabriella, is not somebody you just dreamt up, she was real. Someone you knew when you were younger. Now, you'd been subjected to so much mental abuse, that it's easy to see why you pushed the thoughts of her out your mind. And from what I understand, she was a strong personality in your life. A protector. Just like she is now."

"How do you know?"

"Someone who met you when you were a kid, who is no longer with us told me."

"I don't understand."

Terrell opened his glove compartment and removed a newspaper article with a picture of Gabriella when she was a child along with a sketch drawing.

"Now when you were institutionalized, you helped the artist draw a composite of Gabriella. That's what this picture is," he said handing her the sketch which she remembered.

"How did you get that?"

"It's a long story." He paused. "But look...this is the picture of a girl who went missing from this church." He said pointing at the building. "The resemblance to the sketch and article picture was uncanny."

Yvonna took the pictures and held them side-by-side. And then she looked at his face.

"Are you okay?" He asked lovingly.

Yvonna wiped a tear from her face, looked up to him and said, "She's real. You can actually see the person who has haunted me forever."

"Yes," Terrell smiled as he reached over and touched her shoulder. "She's real."

Yvonna reached over to Terrell and gave him a hug and said, "Thank you so much. You don't know how much this means to me. You can actually see her when nobody else could. What happened to her? Why is this a missing persons picture?"

"It's a long story. But unlike this article says, I have reason to believe that she's still alive, and the information I need is probably in that church. I wanted to bring you here in case you remembered anything."

She looked at it again and said, "Never."

"I'm going to come back here tomorrow, to find out more information. But Yvonna, I'm going to need you to stay low-key. Stay away from Penny and watch everyone new and old in your life. I believe you're surrounded by dangerous people."

"I know."

"But also, there are four people who are trying to kill you who you wouldn't expect. They will stop at nothing to murder you."

"Is one of them my doctor Jona?"

"Just be careful," he warmed. Yvonna had so many people after her that she wasn't surprised anymore. She just felt defeated.

"Do you know them personally, Terrell? The people who are trying to kill me?"

"Yes."

"Please forgive me if this comes out wrong. But...," she said looking down at her baby in her arms, "I started out wanting revenge. I felt there were people I cared about who used me, and I wanted them to pay and most of them have. I even hurt some people in my life that didn't deserve it," she said touching his face softly, "mainly you." She continued.

"But I'm a mother now...who also knows how it feels to be alone. And I don't want that for my baby. I don't want her to have the kind of life I did without knowing a mother's love. So I'm askin' you to do whatever's necessary to keep me safe. I can tell you still love me, and I'm askin' you to prove it."

"Are you saying to me what I think you are?"

"I'm sayin' if you know who wants to hurt me, please take care of them."

Terrell sat back in his seat and examined the most beautiful villainous woman he'd ever met in his life.

"I don't know." He said shaking his head.

"Do it for me." She pleaded. When he seemed hesitant, she placed her baby softly on the back seat of his car. And then she removed her pants.

"What...what are you doing?"

"I'm gonna make love to you," she said climbing softly on top of him.

"This is not what I want."

"I know you want me. I saw it in your eyes the moment I saw you today."

She removed his penis from his pants, and released his thickness. She softly stroked it her hands and bit down on her bottom lip. His body trembled and she knew instantly, how much he still cared about her. Looking at him deeply she said, "Before we make love I need to let you know that I think there's someone else in my life. Someone I care about a lot."

"You love him?" He asked anticipating being inside of her after so long.

"No. But I like him a lot. And the way he argues with me, I think he cares about me too."

Disappointment covered his face. "Have you made love to him yet?"

"No," she smiled kissing his lips softly.

"Then make love to me now," he paused, "and worry about that nigga later."

Terrell pulled her down onto his dick and pumped softly into her waiting body. Yvonna's head dropped back as she kept her moans to a minimum, not wanting to wake Delilah. The wetness from her pussy trickled onto his pants and allowed for an easy entrance. Being overwhelmed with how good she felt, he bit softly on her shoulder.

"Why can't nobody come close to how good you feel?" he asked in a heavy whisper.

She kissed him on the lips breaking any chance he had at speaking again. But this time, unlike the other times they had sex, he wasn't cumming quick. Instead he grabbed her waist and moved her up and down as he met each thrust with passion. Minutes passed and she finally allowed herself to enjoy him, without fear of it ending soon. She needed to be ravished and he was doing exactly that. Her body trembled and her pussy throbbed.

"Damn, Terrell, you makin' me feel so good. I see you got your stamina up." She whispered.

"A lot of shit has changed about me. I'm not the punk I use to be, Yvonna. You changed that about me."

Loving the idea of finally being able to reach an orgasm with him, she rotated her hips so that she could feel him fully. Her soft lips covered his as he suckled her tongue. It was too good to believe, she was about to cum and Terrell was to thank.

"Don't stop," she said a little louder than she wanted. The fact that she couldn't scream because her baby was in the back seat, and that they were in a public parking lot aroused her even more. "Please don't stop. I'm…I'm…about to—,"

Just when she said that, she came all over his stiff dick and he released his cum into her warm body.

"Oh my…oh my…goodness!" she moaned trying to catch her breath. "You don't know how much I needed that."

"And you don't know how much I needed you." He said seriously.

"Don't fall in love with me again, Terrell, I don't wanna hurt you." She saw something familiar in his eyes and it worried her because all she wanted was peace and a chance at a normal life.

"It's too late. I already fell…I just never got up."

"But this is not good. I want to be real wit' you. I'm trying, Terrell."

"Yvonna, I felt guilty for having you and letting you go so easily. I mean, you were the woman who was supposed to be my wife, and I was so consumed with work that I didn't know you were suffering. I never got over the fact that I was your man and a psychiatrist and still didn't know what was going on in my own home. I neglected you," he said smoothing her short hair. "Now I know you have somebody. I get that. But all I'm asking is that you give me a chance to make right the wrongs I did to you in your life. Please, baby. Just one more chance," he said kissing her lips.

"Do you hear yourself?" she said getting off of him putting her clothes back on in an agitated rush. "You always blamin' yourself for shit I do. I hate that about you."

"As well you should, but it doesn't change how I feel. I was your man, and I let you go through this alone. I'm not going to let that happen again, Yvonna. If that nigga you got cares about you, I'm happy for you. I just need you to know that I'm here, no matter what because I still believe you belong to me."

"What about, Jona?"

"I don't love Jona. I never did." He said looking out before him. "I think I fucked with her because of you. It was my sick way of staying connected to someone I still loved. When you got married to Dave, that shit crushed me. I felt it should've been me. To this day I haven't taken your picture off of my desk, that's because I never took you out of my heart."

"I don't know what to say right now." Yvonna said. "I'm not a good person. I don't deserve this kind of love. You're good...and I'm evil. We don't mix well."

"Don't tell me that. We're perfect together. And in time you will see."

THE RIGHT BITCH

"Can I come in?" Yvonna said holding Delilah in her arms.

Bricks rushed up to her and wrapped his arms around her body. "Girl you don't know how fuckin' worried you had me about you." He said closing the door behind them. "You call me and tell me to watch my back and hang up without sayin' shit else."

"I'm sorry. I just had a lot of stuff to think about." She continued placing Delilah down so that she could play with Chomps.

Melvin stood up and said, "Man, I'm 'bout to bounce. I'll get up wit' you later."

He didn't bother speaking to Yvonna. When he left she said, "That's your brother?"

"Yeah."

"Real nice," she said sitting on the sofa.

"We need to talk, Yvonna." He said making no excuse for Melvin. "A lot of shit kicked off today."

"You telling me. Today was the longest day of my life."

"I can believe that. I 'preciate you callin' me 'bout Bet. You were right...she was tryin' to set me up but we took care of it."

"I see you got Chomps." She said looking down at him playing. "What happened?"

"I can't speak on it." He said sitting next to her.

She inhaled and exhaled. "Well, what now?"

"We wait."

"Is that what you wanted to tell me?" she asked looking into his grey eyes.

"No, I wanted to tell you that I care 'bout you."

It was the second time that day she heard that someone cared about her yet she didn't feel worthy. "Bricks, I care 'bout you too. But I'm...I'm not the girlfriend type. I'm loud, mean, heavily opinionated and very vindictive."

"You right about that shit."

"I'm serious." She said looking into his eyes. "I'm all those things but I wanna be different for you. I wanna open my heart to you because I'm tired of not havin' real love." Her body was slumped into the couch and she looked subdued. "I don't wanna fight wit' you no more. I just wanna learn how to love again."

"Damn, ma, I never saw this side of you before." He said as Delilah played with Chomps on the floor.

Then all of a sudden, Delilah bopped Chomps on the head with his own truck and said, "Don't touch!"

"Delilah! Don't do that!" Yvonna said embarrassed.

"Don't worry about it," Bricks said. "They just kids. Look," he pointed at Chomps. "He not even cryin'."

What he said was true about Chomps going on about his business, but what scared Yvonna was the look Delilah had in her eyes. It was undeniably rage and hate mixed and it scared her. But then as if someone flipped on the light switch, she stopped expressing hate and started back playing.

"You okay?" he asked.

"Uh...yeah. I think so." She said examining her baby's strange behavior.

"Where were we?"

She smiled and said, "I wanna be real wit' you. I don't know how this is gonna work out between us, but I'm hopin' you will give me a chance. And that you don't give up on me."

"Naw...I can't do that no more. I'm in it to win it."

"You say that but your actions are different."

"I know. Remember when we was at the club, and I said I wasn't ready for a relationship. I finally get that I wasn't talkin' 'bout you. I'm trynna see if we fit. We been through everything together in these last few days and the only thing I know is that I wanna be wit' you. 'Til death do us part."

Yvonna's heart raced as she thought about her first love Bilal and the tattoo he wore on his arm. It read, 'LalVon' inside a coffin and it meant he and Yvonna 'til death.

She swallowed hard and said, "So you sayin' you really wanna give us a chance?"

"I'm sayin' I need to be wit' you. So what you wanna do?"

Just when he said that, Tina knocked on the door and Bricks let her in. "Hey, cuzo, I'm here to get Chomps." She said looking at Yvonna. "Hey, Yvonna."

Yvonna waved and said, "Hi, Tina."

"Can I wrap to you for a second, Bricks?" Tina said turning back around to face Yvonna. "Alone."

Bricks looked at Yvonna and said, "Gimmie a sec." He saw the seriousness in his cousin's eyes as they walked into the kitchen. "What up? You cool?"

"Carmen's at my house," she said in a low voice, "she said she was sposed to be stayin' with you for two weeks and that she flew all the way up here from Georgia. Had it been any other bitch I would've sent her on her way but I know you fucks wit' her like that. So what you want me to do?"

Bricks walked away from his cousin and leaned up against the refrigerator. The Captain Crunch cereal box fell off the top and hit the floor. With all of the drama, he had forgotten to tell Carmen not to come. And now that he had fallen for a woman he hadn't even fucked, he had forgotten all about her.

"You forgot didn't you?" He nodded in agreement. "What you want me to tell her, Bricks? I can get rid of her if you want. Just say the word. She came on the block but you know they wouldn't let her on the street without approval. So she called me like all your chicks do and now I got her up in my crib. But it ain't nothin' to get rid of her either."

"Naw...don't do that," he said as he put his hands in his face and dropped them by his sides. "Let me talk to Yvonna first. I'll call you later."

"You sure?" She asked with raised eyebrows. "Don't mess your thing up here if you don't have too."

"Naw. Let me wrap to my peoples and I'll call you." He confirmed.

"Cool." Tina said as she grabbed Chomps and walked out the door. With Chomps gone, Delilah was happy to have full reign of the floor and appeared unmoved by his absence.

When they were alone Yvonna said, "Look, I was thinking about making us a nice little dinner tonight. Just the three of us now since Chomps gone. Since we gonna be up in the house waiting to get rid of Swoopes ass for

235

three weeks. I might as well show you my cookin' skills."

Bricks sat down next to her on the couch and allowed the seriousness of what he was about to say to show on his face. He placed one hand on her knee and said, "Look, before me and you started kickin' it, I told somebody I would be wit' them today and I forgot about it."

"Okay...is it a...girl?" she asked hoping it wasn't the case.

"Yea."

Realizing she'd just been with Terrell a few moments earlier she decided not to be stupid and immature about the matter. I mean Bricks was fine and he was bound to have someone around who wanted him. But she really liked Bricks and wanted things to work out between them too. "Okay, I'll give you tonight. But tomorrow you mine." She smiled trying to take it all in. "So you have to let her know."

"Actually, she's here for two weeks."

"Two weeks? This sounds serious. What about all that you love the single life shit? I mean...why wouldn't you tell me 'bout her?"

"It's not like that, Squeeze. For real! I'm not a cruddy nigga so I can't just send her back home on a plane to Atlanta. The girl came all this way to see me and I was so caught up with this drama and Swoopes, that I didn't catch her in time. The girl wanted to be wit' me and I fucked up."

"And so do I. I wanna be wit' you too, Bricks. Don't do this to me."

"I can't leave the girl stranded, Yvonna. I have to say something to her."

"Why can't you leave her stranded?" she frowned. "You was about to kick me and my baby to the curb the other night. What's the difference?"

"Let me take care of this situation and I promise, we can work it out. I just don't want us to start off wrong."

"Do you like her?" He didn't respond. "You like her. Oh my God I'm such a fuckin' fool!"

"Yvonna stop trippin'! I'm starting to believe you really are crazy." That hurt her more than he could ever know.

"You know what," she said grabbing her baby, "fuck you and fuck this house!"

"I'm sorry! I shouldna said that."

"I shared something with you that fucks wit' me every day and you threw it in my face! You ain't nothin' but a bum as nigga!"

"I said I was sorry but look how you actin'!"

"How you sound, Bricks? The one nigga I try to give my heart to for real runs games on me. Maybe I'm more woman than you can handle. After all, you was fuckin' wit' a bitch wit' rubber titties." Just when she said that, a light bulb went off in her head. "Or was it a man? You fuckin' men now, Bricks?"

"Fuck you, bitch! I want you out my fuckin' house!"

"Tell me somethin' you haven't said twenty times already, fuckin' faggot!"

"If you didn't have that baby wit' you, I'd drop your ass."

"And you'd get dropped back, bitch ass nigga!" She screamed.

He looked at Delilah and stomped down the stairs, slamming the door behind him. But the moment he hit the bottom step, something in his body told him something wasn't right. He hadn't been in the basement since he came home with Melvin and that was a bad move.

"What's up, Bricks?" Swoopes said holding a gun with a silencer attached. "Fancy meeting you here."

Bricks had left his weapon on the table upstairs, a move he'd soon regret. "Sounds like you're having a lover's spat upstairs. Ya'll cool?"

"You not gonna make it outta here alive."

"Sure I will. You see, you just got into it wit' Yvonna so your family's going to think she did it. I mean, ain't you got some broad you bringing over here later?" he smiled. "That would be a perfect reason for Yvonna to kill you."

"They not gonna believe that shit."

"Sure they will. And just like earlier when your whole crew left the block to protect you when you went to Bet's hotel, they gonna all leave to go find Yvonna. And I'll walk out as smoothly as I came in. And then I'ma sit in the cut and wait for your family to kill Yvonna for me. I was hoping to get both of you myself but this is better. It's the perfect plan."

Bricks was about to lunge at him when Swoopes unloaded four bullets silently into his chest. And as he did earlier, Swoopes hid within the darkness of the basement.

Upstairs Yvonna didn't hear a thing and was too busy caught up in her rage. Once she picked up her things, she grabbed her baby and ran into Melvin on the way out of Brick's house.

"You leaving so early?" he asked speaking to her for the first time.

"Don't worry, I'm not fuckin' wit' your brother ever again!" She yelled. "So you don't have to worry 'bout me!"

Melvin looked at her, shook his head and walked into the house. "That bitch crazy." He said walking inside, only to find his brother slumped on the basement floor.

KNIGHT AND SHINING DOCTOR

Yvonna woke up the next morning with an extreme headache. But luckily for her, she had doctor Terrell to take care of her. He had gotten a nice hotel for she and Delilah and he stayed with them. He knew Jona would be angry but he no longer gave a fuck about her and wasn't playing games. He wanted to be with Yvonna and that was the bottom line.

"You hungry?" he asked rolling over to kiss her softly on the lips.

"Yes. And can you get me some Tylenol too? I have a terrible headache."

Terrell kissed her gently on the face, got dressed and fetched her food and medicine. The moment he left the room, she reached for her cell phone. Although she knew she wasn't supposed to power it on, because Swoopes could track her, she still wanted to see if Bricks called. She missed him already and hoped he missed her too. When the phone was on, she saw she had five missed voice messages. Three were from a funny number with the plus symbol between the digits and she knew immediately it was Ming calling from China. She decided to listen to hers first.

"You must call, Ming as soon as possible. My uncle told me of great problem in New York and he's very angry with me."

The second message said, *"Do you know where Darcus is? Ming must speak to one of you right away. This is serious."*

The third message said, *"Ming is on her way home from China. Please be at my house by 12:00am. We must speak. Uncle Yao is very angry."*

After she listened to those messages she listened to a fourth message where her sister was crying uncontrollably on the phone. She made mental notes to put her at ease about their argument, after she got a new phone.

But it was the fifth message that caused her heart to jump out of her chest.

"For what you did to my brother, bitch, you gonna pay. You betta jump off of a bridge because it'll be easier than what I'm gonna do to you."

She leaped off of the bed and paced the floor. She had no idea what he was talking about but she knew whatever happened, Melvin thought she was to blame. Could this mean something happened to Bricks between the time she last saw him and the morning? But how could it? He had 24-hour security at all times protecting him. So she made one last call to Tina.

"What do you want?" Tina said evilly.

"Listen, I don't know what's going on, but I would never do anything to hurt Bricks and I know you know that. So can you please tell me what's happening?"

Tina paused and said, "He was shot." Yvonna felt for a wall behind her where there was none and stumbled to the floor. "And Melvin said you were the last one who saw him, and that you were mad at him when you left his house."

"Please...please tell me this isn't true." She sobbed unable to defend herself against the impossible accusation. She had killed a lot of people in her day, but she never wanted to do anything but love Bricks. "I need for you to tell me that this isn't true, Tina. Tell me somebody didn't hurt my Bricks."

"I wish it wasn't true," she cried, "but it is."

"Is he...is he..." the words couldn't leave her mouth. "Is he...dead?"

"No." Yvonna exhaled and thanked God for the huge favor. "Where is he?"

"Why should I trust you?"

"Because I love him. And if you guys think I did hurt him, it will be easier for you to get me if I turn myself over to you. I just need to see his face. Please." Tina didn't need convincing, she believed her the moment she called.

"We at the Washington Hospital Center. Room 318."

"I'm on my way."

Yvonna told Terrell she had something to do and begged him to care for Delilah and he gladly obliged. She ran into the hospital and onto the wing where Bricks was. The moment she hit the floor, there were about thirty people in attendance leaning on the hospital walls all there for Bricks. And they all had one thing in common, extreme hate for Yvonna. They lined the walls until she got closer to Bricks room. Standing up straight they turned toward her ready to attack. But there was one person in particular, someone she hadn't seen before, who raised his shirt showing the handle of his weapon that frightened her. On his arm was a tattoo that read, 'Kelsi AKA K-Man loves you Ma. RIP.'

Kelsi was just about to blast on her when Melvin said, "Leave her alone. She's mine."

Standing beside Kelsi was a pretty girl with almond colored skin and a thick body. Yvonna knew she was the girl who came to visit Bricks. Not caring who was present she walked up to Melvin with blood red eyes and fell at his feet. "Kill me!" she sobbed. "I'm so fuckin' tired of death that I don't care about my life anymore." Her stomach jerked so much that it knotted up in pain. "I love him too, Melvin! And I would never do anything to hurt him. Not Bricks. I'm sorry for bringing Swoopes into his life. Please forgive me or kill me." Melvin looked down at her and out at his family.

"Why is she here?" Carmen asked crying too. "This is all her fault!"

"You don't know shit about me!" Yvonna stood up and walked over to her. "I've been through more shit wit' that man than you'll ever know!"

Kelsi put his hand out in front of him and said, "I don't know what's goin' on, but my peoples in there fucked up and I ain't feelin' this soap opera shit. So I'ma need you to back the fuck up before you get me outta character."

Yvonna turned around to Melvin and said, "It wasn't me. I need you to know that it wasn't me."

The moment he looked into her eyes, he knew that she couldn't possibly hurt Bricks. He was just about to speak when Tina ran into the hallway from Brick's room and said, "He opened his eyes. He opened his eyes!"

Although everyone had a head start to get into the

room before her, Yvonna was able to wiggle herself to his bedside. There were so many people inside the small space that you could barely see the white walls. But when Bricks eye's focused he saw Yvonna and reached out for her.

"Squeeze," she gripped his hand. "Do...y...you know h...how much shit you got me into?"

Yvonna couldn't laugh and instead she burst into tears. "I'm sooo sorry, baby. I never meant for this to happen."

"I'm, okay." When she wouldn't stop crying he grabbed her hand as hard as he could and said, "I'm okay. But I need you to listen," he whispered. "You...gotta be careful. The only thing that kept me alive was thinking 'bout you and I can't stand to lose you again." Hearing that, Carmen stormed out of the room.

"Excuse me!" the doctor yelled from the doorway. "I have to see the patient and there are too many people in here. He suffered severe wounds to his chest cavity and could have died! I must check on him. Please get out of my way."

"Calm down, doc," Melvin said placing a hand firmly on his shoulder. "This a family matter so give us one minute."

The frightened white doctor said, "Okay. One minute and then you're all out of here!"

Melvin shooed him away and said, "The bitch ass doctor gonna put us out. But before I leave, I need to know what happened."

"Swoopes." He said looking up at Melvin. "He...he was in the house when we came home from Bet's hotel and I ain't know. He was in there when the ambulance came to get me too. I tried to tell ya'll but the words couldn't come out."

Melvin's eyebrows pulled together and his face hardened. "That nigga was in your crib while I was there?" He said hitting his chest.

Bricks had already used up more of his energy than he had in him to speak so he nodded instead. Thinking of almost losing Bricks because of Swoopes once again, caused a fury to brew inside of Yvonna. Transformed she turned around and rushed out of the room.

"M...Melvin, don't let him hurt her." Bricks said reaching out for him. "Don't let him kill my shawty. Watch her for me...P...please."

"You know I got it lil brah."

Melvin tried his best to keep up with her but Yvonna couldn't be caught. Her feet caught wheels as she ran out of the hospital. There was so much rage in her heart that she could taste how good it would feel to kill Swoopes. But when she walked out of the hospital door, someone was waiting on her instead.

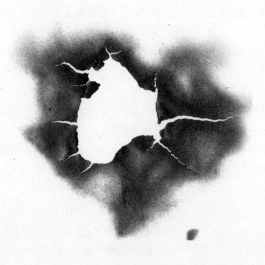

UNCLE YAO

A black Lincoln Navigator Limousine covered the entrance of the hospital. It was the same limo that visited Ming right down to the driver with the missing ear.

"Yvonna," the well-dressed driver said, "Uncle Yao wants to speak to you. Please, come inside."

Yvonna's heart paced as she thought about how she could get out of the offer. She soon realized she couldn't. "I...really can't come now. Maybe I can make an appointment with him later."

"You can, and you will see him now," the driver said. "Next time I won't ask so nicely."

Yvonna eased inside and saw a handsome older Chinese man wearing a crisp black designer suit. She was also surprised to see that the inside of the limo was completely white. "So...you drink?" Uncle Yao asked in a thick accent.

"No." Yvonna said sliding into one of the plush leather seats.

"You do today," he said as the driver pulled off.

Yvonna accepted the drink and ran her finger around the rim of the glass. "So...I hear great things about you from my niece." He said with a smile. "And then, I hear bad things about you from my New York friend. Why is that?"

She was debating on whether to lie to a man that she was certain could read her mind. "Darcus did something to the package before he took it to the connect. I think he did it at a truck stop and I knew something wasn't right, so I snapped a picture of him going inside with the bag. I overheard him later saying to someone on the phone how he could sell the packages himself. So when he didn't come back out after the drop, I got scared and left. I found the packages he stuffed under the seat, and have them right here," she said holding her purse.

Yao extended his hands and she gave them to him. "You are good liar." Yvonna's mouth dropped in surprise that he found her out. "But you're really cunning. To think you can think of such a ridiculous story, and that I'd believe you, makes you valuable to me. You virtually without fear, although you shouldn't be."

"What do you mean?"

"Do you know who I am?"

"Yes."

"Do you know how dangerous I am?"

"I've heard how dangerous you can be."

"Good, then I don't have to spend a lot of time telling you how serious I am. I get what I want, and what I want is for you to work for me. To kill for me when I need you. You can get into places I can't by your looks and your ability to seduce."

"What? I can't do that. I'm a mother and I have to care for my daughter."

"So you don't want to be alive long enough to see her grow?" he asked shooting her an evil stare.

"Yes. Yes. I do."

"Good."

Yvonna looked out of the window and stared back at him. She hated being forced to do anything and she was beyond angry. "Is that all?"

"No. Darcus was delivered to us, alive by my New York friend. And before I killed him personally, he left this message for you."

Yao removed a white paper from his pocket. Within it was another paper with a number on it. It was stained in blood. Yvonna immediately recognized the number and felt a jolt pierce through her stomach. She had left that number next to her husband Dave's bedside, the day she killed him in Jamaica. She was trying to throw the Jamaican police off of her trail, by setting the weed connect up instead. That connect was Darcus.

"He said, '*Yvonna, I underestimated you, and for that, I will pay with me life. You framed me twice in this lifetime. First for the murder of your husband Dave, in me country Jamaica, and second with our trip to New York. I was locked up for two years in Jamaica, until they finally realized there wasn't enough evidence to hold me. I never told them 'bout you, because I wanted you for meself. And although I didn't get me vengeance now, I will most certainly see you in hell.*'

"Believe it or not," Yao started, "before we took this letter from him, I was going to kill you too. Because like I said, I believe you are involved. But, when on his dying day he chose not to speak to a member of family, as is tradition in my country, but to write letter to you instead, it intrigued me. Greatly. I'm sure we will work good together. And I'm going to teach you everything there is to know about Wushu and how to kill without a trace. You will be my prodigy."

Yvonna was speechless. She would have never guessed that the man, who shared a bed with her on a night she couldn't remember, was also the man she tried to frame for her husband's death.

"You might as well ask him to take care of Swoopes," Gabriella said sitting next to her. "I think he sees your value and would do anything to keep you. Work it for what you can."

"Uncle Yao," Yvonna said seductively.

"Please...call me Yao." He said flirtatiously.

"Yao...I have someone I need you to take care of, if I'm gonna be a good employee I can't worry about him hurting people I love."

Yao smiled and said, "Always the cunning one. Give me his name and we will rid you of him immediately."

"Thank you," She smiled and sat back in her seat.

She couldn't wait to see the look on his face, when he discovered she had China on her side.

A MONTH LATER

Yvonna sat in her expensive condominium overlooking Baltimore city in a development called Silo Point. The sun lit up the water and sparkled against the windows of the buildings. She exhaled and took in what was the beginning of her new life.

After all of the drama with Swoopes, she was in need of a change of address. As she walked onto her balcony, she tugged at her designer pink robe and smiled. She was really on top of the world.

"What you lookin' at baby?" Bricks asked walking up behind her, placing his arms around her waist.

"The city. I didn't even know Baltimore could be so pretty."

"Yeah...I can't believe you moved all the way out here. You know us D.C. boys don't get down wit' these Baltimore cats like that."

"Are you sure you don't rep Bmore now instead? You be here every day."

He laughed and said, "I walked right into that. But

look," he said releasing her. "I gotta go. Have you given any thought to us? Workin' at it again?"

"Bricks, I think it's best if we remain friends. It seems everybody I care about, gets hurt one way or another."

"You say that shit, but your eyes say somethin' different, Yvonna. That shit that happened to me was not your fault. And I'm still here."

"For now, friends, Bricks. Okay?"

She hugged him tightly and he gripped her waist. "Stop playin' fuckin' games wit' me. You know what's up wit' us. And I'll be here later to discuss our future. Right now I gotta roll."

Yvonna walked him out and fell up against the door. She had fallen for Bricks and she was afraid to love him. After he got shot, she blamed herself for it even though he begged her not too. A week later, she said all she could offer him was friendship at least that way she'd know he would be safe.

Walking into her large living room, she plopped onto her white designer couch and picked up her phone to call her best friend. She had finally got use to Yvonna and Yao working together despite hating it at first.

"Hey, what time you come by?" Ming asked. "Delilah not playing with Boy very nicely today."

"What do you mean?"

"She smacked Boy in face and took his Jade bracelet! Your daughter's mean."

"I'm sorry, she has been gettin' more violent lately. But they are brother and sister, Ming. Maybe it's just that kinda feud between 'em." Yvonna offered.

"Ming don't think so."

"Aight, can you give me a few hours?"

"Yes…but hurry!"

She wanted to get Delilah but she also knew she had

work to do later that evening. Yao had finally gained ground in D.C.'s cocaine market, and was met with one problem and he wanted Yvonna to make that problem go away. That problem was Mom's, who would be murdered that evening at 8:00 PM.

Picking up the phone once more, she called Terrell. They had gotten closer too but she couldn't commit to him either. She was starting to believe that she was meant to be alone.

"Terrell, how are you?" Yvonna said sipping her cold water with strawberries and ice floating around inside of her glass.

"I'm fine. I was just about to call you to remind you about our lunch date. We're still on right?"

"Yes."

"Good, because I know you're going to China for three months tomorrow. Even though you never told me what you're going to do there."

She couldn't tell him that she would have to endure a long arduous training in Wushu and weaponry. When she'd come back, she'd truly be one of the most deadly women alive.

"Okay...well I'll see you in a few hours. I have something planned I know you're going to love."

"I could use some fun."

"Later, Yvonna. I love you," he paused. "And you don't have to say it back."

What Terrell already knew was that she hadn't planned to.

KINDRED SPIRITS

Yvonna sat inside Tea Love, a quaint little restaurant in Baltimore City that specialized in various assortments of teas. But she decided on an alcoholic drink to relax her mind. Certain he was going to ask her to be with him again, she wanted to be calm when she said no. "Anything else, mam?" the waiter asked.

"No...I'm just waiting on a friend."

Five minutes later, Terrell walked through the door. Sporting a beige sports coat, it looked smooth against his permanent bronze complexion. Whenever he walked into a room she forgot how fine he was, until she laid eyes on him again. But there was someone walking next to him that caused Yvonna to shoot out of her seat, knocking over the chair behind her.

What was going on? She'd gone to her new doctor, and was taking a medicine she was sure was working. One that didn't make her sleepy like the other medications did. So she couldn't understand why, Gabriella was walking in the door beside Terrell.

"Yvonna?" Terrell said picking up the chair behind her, while Gabriella stood across the table before her. "Are you okay?"

"Yes." She said trying to ignore Gabriella. She figured if she didn't focus on her, she'd go away. "I'm fine."

"Are you sure?" he said softly placing his hand in the small of her back.

"Yes." She swallowed hard. "Yes I am."

"Good...because this is the surprise I had for you. This is the person I wanted you to meet. Again." He had broken into the church and found the box containing Gabriella's address. It was difficult to find at first, until he remembered Dmitry saying that the pastor had a non-profit organization in her name. Going through that file, he found everything he needed to know about Gabriella, including her address.

"You mean, she's actually there?" Outside of her hair being long, she looked the exact same way Yvonna envisioned her in her mind.

"Yes." She said her voice as smooth as the strum of a guitar. "I'm real...and you don't know how good it feels to see and speak to you again." A tear fell down her face. "Because..." she said in a deep low hush. "There's so much I have to talk to you about. So much you have to be afraid of," she said looking around. "lives are in danger. Both of ours."

THE FINAL MEETING

"Did Terrell say what he wanted?" Lily asked Guy who was sitting at the table as usual, eating pizza.

"Nope. He didn't call me, he sent me a text message."

"Well...did he tell you what it was about?" Lily questioned. "Because all I got was a text message too. Telling us to meet him here."

Jona rose from a sitting position on the bed and said, "This doesn't feel right. I haven't spoken to Terrell since he left me three months ago. And now, he has asked to meet with us, although he spoke to no one personally."

As Lily grabbed the bottle of bourbon from the table, and poured it into the cheap paper cup, a bullet ripped through it splattering the brown liquid onto her white shirt. A second bullet followed and killed the lights. The glass in the window was shattered completely and in walked a sleek woman, dressed in all black with a facemask on. Behind her were two other men, holding weapons.

Removing her mask, Yvonna smiled at them all. They could see her face through the lights from the shattered window.

"I see you got my message," she said smiling at all of

them. "You should've killed me while you had the chance. Now it's too late."

Walking back out of the window she placed her hand on one of her men's shoulder and said, "Finish them, boys."

Epilogue

Three months after Bricks was shot, Kendal's body showed up in an abandoned car in a D.C. project. She was shot once in the head and was naked from head to toe. And Bricks maintained sole custody of Chomps.

Penny waged a war against Yvonna by filing for custody of her daughter Delilah. She lost with the court finding she had no legal right to the child. Terrell was made Delilah's guardian in the event something happened to Yvonna. The child's father, who was still paralyzed from the neck down, wanted nothing to do with her.

Jesse and Yvonna continued to work at their relationship and they were growing stronger together. And although Jesse never fully trusted her, they were closer than ever before.

Swoopes was never found. After learning that Yvonna was working with Yao, he packed up and moved out of town after losing Growl and most of his men to Yao's acts of violence. Through it all the very woman who he abused, Crystal, stood by his side and went on the run with him.

Three months after leaving he sent message through Crystal to Yvonna. He let her know that he had no intentions on going too far, until he got a chance to spit on her grave.

Delilah, as she grew she started showing a propensity for violence. Yvonna tried not to worry, but it was hard to deny, that the traits she'd become accustomed to, were taking their toll on her daughter. But for now she was a child, and all Yvonna could do was pray that she'd outgrow the very attributes that made Yvonna Harris the most hated woman alive.

COMING SOON

Shyt List IV

The Cartel Collection
Established in January 2008
We're growing stronger by the month!!!
www.thecartelpublications.com

Cartel Publications Order Form
Inmates <u>ONLY</u> get novels for $10.00 per book!

Titles		*Fee*
Shyt List	_____	$15.00
Shyt List 2	_____	$15.00
Pitbulls In A Skirt	_____	$15.00
Pitbulls In A Skirt 2	_____	$15.00
Victoria's Secret	_____	$15.00
Poison	_____	$15.00
Poison 2	_____	$15.00
Hell Razor Honeys	_____	$15.00
Hell Razor Honeys 2	_____	$15.00
A Hustler's Son 2	_____	$15.00
Black And Ugly As Ever	_____	$15.00
Year of The Crack Mom	_____	$15.00
The Face That Launched a Thousand Bullets	_____	$15.00
The Unusual Suspects	_____	$15.00
Miss Wayne & The Queens of DC	_____	$15.00
Year of The Crack Mom	_____	$15.00
Familia Divided	_____	$15.00
Shyt List III	_____	$15.00
Raunchy	_____	$15.00
Reversed	_____	$15.00

Please add $2.00 per book for shipping and handling.
The Cartel Publications * P.O. Box 486 * Owings Mills * MD * 21117

Name: _____

Address:_____

City/State:_____

Contact # & Email:_____

Please allow 5-7 business days for delivery. The Cartel is not responsible for prison orders rejected.

CARTEL PUBLICATIONS TITLES

THE CARTEL street team
makin' this shit look too good...

Wanna earn some extra cash?
Join our street team and find out how!!!

Visit: www.thecartelpublications.com for more information.